*Real love.*

His skin was tanned red-brown, the deep red-brown that is the color of buffalo-calf fur in the autumn. Slim with rope-tight muscles, he rode his horse bareback. A light seemed to shine in his eyes, and there was a hint of a smile at the ends of his long, thin mouth as he looked down at me. Favorite-Child threw more berries and kept screaming with laughter, even at Eagle-Sun. But I did not dare.

I was silent and watched him. He was silent and watched me.

*point*

# SWEETGRASS

*Jan Hudson*

SCHOLASTIC INC.

New York Toronto London Auckland Sydney
Mexico City New Delhi Hong Kong Buenos Aires

AUTHOR'S NOTE:

I would like to thank all those who helped in the long process of creating this novel, either with the history behind it or the actual manuscript: Bill and Donna Howse, Ernie Hudson, Art Lamothe, Caroline Heath, Joyce Green, Esther Tailfeathers, and the helpful staff of the University of Calgary library and the Glenbow Museum. Special thanks are due to John Wright, Jeanne Henry, and the late Laurence G. Wiedrick (my father), all of the University of Alberta.

Tree Frog Press would also like to thank Theresa Ford, Jeanne Henry, Joanne Lynes, Lorla Wasmuth, Harry Savage, David May, Sheryl Brook, Fiona MacGregor, Al Granger, the Canadian Library Association, the Canada Council, the Film & Literary Arts Branch of Alberta Culture, Grant Kennedy of Lone Pine Publishing, and the Alberta Foundation for the Literary Arts.

10          23          10 09

*To my almost-daughter, Cindy Lynn,*
*wishing her strength from each of her inheritances,*
*and to the Blackfoot historical novelists of the future.*

The people in this story are not historical personages,
but fictional creations. The events, however, are based on
written records of the Blackfoot Indians during the
winter of 1837 to 1838. The Blackfoots, also known as
Siksika, occupied the territory that is now northern Montana,
and southern and south central Alberta, Canada.

# CONTENTS

# 1

## SUMMER BERRIES

"WHAT DO YOU MEAN, PRETTY-GIRL?" I ASKED AS WE gathered strawberries that early summer morning. "Who could your parents want you to marry except Shy-Bear?"

"They will not say who they have chosen for me. Probably some old man. And everyone will shame me for not being happy to marry."

It was still exciting—my first friend-to-be-married! Pretty-Girl could not know how I would have sacrificed a finger to be in her place. I was fifteen, and she was thirteen—but she was the one whose parents had announced her marriage.

"But you and your Shy-Bear have cared for each other for two summers. Almost as long as I have cared for Eagle-Sun. And everyone has seen you together. Your parents must have noticed; everyone else has."

I sighed with happiness as we picked the small, fragrant berries. We had to be careful or else the strawberry blood would stain this perfect day. Sun, sand, sage and small red berries—a bird sang to us from a rosebrush clump, joyfully—the pattern of our lives.

All things moved as they should. Our lives seemed fixed as in a beaded design or the roundness of an old tale told on winter nights. Time would soon make women of us in marriage.

A few details of Pretty-Girl's story still sounded a little odd to me, though.

"Exactly what did your mother and father say to you?" I asked.

"Father said nothing. Mother told me. She just said that I should start sewing a new pair of moccasins, right for a bride."

"And then?"

"And then she said she would make a good new dress. Then she went out of the tipi. Nothing more, Sweetgrass."

How dully she said it. Pretty-Girl kept picking the strawberries as steady as could be. Her little hands pulled at them as daintily as a deer plucking grass in a meadow. She had big eyes like a deer too, and beautiful long hair. I wished I looked like that.

"Don't you understand, Sweetgrass? My parents will not give me to Shy-Bear."

"Why not? You should ask them." I reached out and touched her shoulder. "Tell them—"

She shrugged my hand off. "You know how poor my family is. Shy-Bear does not have half the horses Father could get for me from some older man."

"Pretty-Girl—"

"Some older man with ten wives already, I bet that is what has been chosen for me!" The words tumbled out of her. "I will be the slavewife and clean buffalo hides all day and do all the hardest work. No one will ever be kind to me. Everything will always be awful until the babies come and even then it will still be bad. How I wish I did not have to. Oh, I would rather be dead than married!"

Tears fell on the berries. Tears are the wrong way to greet the marriage that every Blackfoot girl longs for. What could I say to make her act the right way?

"So your parents are giving you a new dress to go to your husband in. How lucky you are!"

Pretty-Girl said nothing.

"What kind of decorations are on the dress? Did your mother say?"

My friend looked up. She had decided not to cry, after all.

"What difference does the dress make? I want to know *who* I am going to wear it for!" She hid her face again.

I thought quickly. "Shy-Bear went on that horse raid against the Crows the sun before last and will be back soon."

"But he will not be able to bring back enough horses."

"Well, even so, you will not be treated like a slavewife. A new wife, perhaps. Especially one as beautiful as you."

"No?"

"How could anyone not love and honor you more than his other wives? You are as beautiful as a great chief's daughter in an old story. Remember all the things men have given to beautiful women. . . ."

"It will not happen. This is not a story."

"Of course it will. Please feel better now." I gave her a hug. All her sorrow made me feel strange inside.

"You do not understand, Sweetgrass. You are spoiled."

Spoiled? I always hear this. My almost-mother Bent-Over-Woman says Father gives me too much attention because I am his only daughter. Aside from my obnoxious almost-brother Otter, now twelve summers old, there have only been babies in our tipi. And when they die young, they are not counted. This is supposed to explain why my father lets me do what I want most of the time. A good Blackfoot girl is always obedient, quiet, hard-working, and she never says what she feels.

When I say what I feel, my father just laughs at me. My mother, people have said, was Father's favorite of the three sisters he married. Who knows if that is so? I was only a baby when she died, too young to know anything. Only Almost-Mother is left now and she never talks about her sisters.

And Father gives me all the little things I want.

But he only gives me the little things—never the big ones. In important things like marriage, my parents treat me like a child. But I will be sixteen next summer. Then I will probably be the oldest unmarried girl among all the Bloods—even among all three Blackfoot tribes together—if Father does not stop finding excuses to keep me at home!

I stood up and pulled a flowering blade of sweetgrass from a little clump. That is my name, Sweetgrass. It is ordinary to look at, but it is as fragrant as the spring.

Sun shone on us. "Take this," I said to Pretty-Girl.

She twirled the grass in her hand, half-smiling, then tucked it into her thick hair and pulled some more for me. I wove them into my braids. My hair was burning hot and the sweetgrass sent out a dizzying perfume into the morning air.

"My father will arrange a marriage for me, too. Maybe this summer at the Sun Dance. Next summer for sure."

"Perhaps," said Pretty-Girl.

"Next summer, you will see. You and I will climb from the river together to pick strawberries, and we will be carrying our own babies on our backs. We will tell each other about our husbands and the fine horses that they own."

Promises hung shimmering in the future like glowing berries above sandy soil as we gathered our bags for the walk home. We had to hurry as the warriors would be back soon.

Many tipis, maybe even twenty, stood below us on the green campsite. My people were gathering together on their way to the Sun Dance. Oh, summer is the best time of the year!

I sang a little and Pretty-Girl smiled at me. I smiled back. She looked happy now.

"I would bet if you look at your husband with your big eyes . . ." I began.

"You would bet on anything," laughed Pretty-Girl. "Worse than your almost-brother, Otter. You will lose everything you own someday."

"Never!"

"Yes, you will. Was it not an uncle of yours who lost his last horse playing knucklebone and then had to walk until someone lent him another?"

She distracted me by leaning over to poke at a big crumbling skull half-buried in the soft clay. You will often see that kind of bone in the Red Deer River badlands. Bigger than buffalo bones, and heavy. Almost like rocks.

And eerie.

"Pretty-Girl! Stay away from those old bones."

"Would not the people of the old-time feast well on buffalo this size?" she mused. "Maybe old-time people killed them for their Sun Dance."

"My grandmother says when her mother was young, there was no Sun Dance at all."

"Then where did all our heroes get their power, if not from their offerings to Sun? In the old times, I mean. Who but Sun would give them victory? There must have been a Sun Dance."

All I wanted to think about was the next Sun Dance. Soon my sweetheart, my hoped-to-be-sweetheart, would ride down from the north to brighten my days. Our camp would join his, almost any day now. Hurry faster, Eagle-Sun.

I slipped into a daydream and didn't even notice how far we had walked until Pretty-Girl grabbed my arm.

"Look, Sweetgrass! Look!"

She was pointing to the jagged horizon.

I squinted into the light and saw our returning warriors galloping their horses down the cliff path.

Their hair was flowing in the wind, colored streamers flying from horses and men alike. Brown arms were raised in victory. We could faintly hear the screams of the captured stallions and mares driven ahead of the raiders. The young men's bodies were graceful mysteries in their distance and in their power.

"A good raid!" I cried. Many horses rode with them, many horses to repay the older men who had helped start their careers. Many horses, at last, to pay a father to soften the loss of his young daughter in marriage.

"No one is hurt," Pretty-Girl breathed, "or they would not be racing, would they?"

"Of course not!"

Otter had gone on his first horse raid with Five-Killer's nephew, Open-Metal. What nerve in one so young! I hurried faster without admitting I cared how my almost-brother had done.

"Hurry," I cried. Pretty-Girl laughed a little as she jogged the few steps to catch up. I continued my reassurances. "I bet if you look at your man with those big eyes of yours and laugh like that, and let him smell the sweetgrass in your hair, I bet he will *have* to love you."

I heard a shout and turned to see Pretty-Girl sprawling on the ground. She had slipped in the soft clay.

"Father will marry me to Five-Killer," she wept. "I saw Five-Killer's nephew, the one who went on the raid."

"So?"

"So he was tying the best horses to Five-Killer's tipi. I just now saw it, in my mind. Father will want those beautiful horses more than anything. He'll marry me to Five-Killer and that is all."

It was a true omen. Pretty-Girl saw it and she felt it inside her. That was what was going to be.

After all, I breathed silently to myself, nothing very bad could happen. And the worst that could happen to Pretty-Girl could not happen to me. Despite her beauty, she was *kimataps*—from a poor family. But my father had been a celebrated warrior when he was young, until his leg was permanently injured from being thrown by his horse one day on a hunting expedition. Everyone knew

· 15 ·

the proud name of Shabby-Bull. He would never make his only daughter a slavewife, no matter how many horses he was offered.

I would make Father do what I wanted. I would find the signs, the power to control my own days. I would make my life be what I wanted.

# 2

## EAGLE-SUN'S RETURN

WE FOUND THE RAIDING PARTY EASILY, BY FOLLOWING the noise of neighing horses and excited shouts to a clot of people at the camp's center. There the victorious young men of our band and Five-Killer's band walked their new horses back and forth with smug dignity. Everyone was praising them. My almost-brother Otter was nowhere in sight.

I felt a gentle poke in my ribs. "Ask if all the raiders came back safely," Pretty-Girl whispered.

But who? Ah, there. One figure stood lonely on the edge of the commotion, an old widow. She was one of my relatives and would be friendly to us.

"Arrow-Meat-Woman," I asked, "can you tell us if anyone was hurt in the raid?"

"No one was wounded . . . umm . . . or just one young man was. Now who was it?" Her face wrinkled even more.

I stood respectfully silent, looking at the ground. No matter what my almost-mother says, I behave as a good, polite Blackfoot girl should.

Behind me Pretty-Girl swung her berry bags, bumping me on the backs of my knees.

"A young man I do not know."

Pretty-Girl couldn't wait any longer. "Please," she begged, "it was not Shy-Bear, was it?"

The old widow's clouded eyes blinked. "No, not Shy-Bear."

Pretty-Girl sighed with relief.

"You girls need not worry. It was no one of importance, just some pup from a *kimataps* family."

We said our thanks and left.

Pretty-Girl slid ahead of me into the crowd, in and out like a ribbon through hair. I followed her. People were laughing and talking all around us. Maybe there would be a victory feast tonight. Where was my friend going? She was looking anxiously into each face as she came across it, but in one direction she made a point of not looking. There Chief Five-Killer stood talking with some of the raiders.

I looked at Five-Killer. He stood tall and well-bodied, his face stern like the stone face of a mountain, the way an important man should be. He did not seem that old. He stood well. Everyone watched him and listened to his praise of his modest young nephew who had stolen the fine horses.

Pretty-Girl did not have much luck looking for her sweetheart. I did not see Otter, either, so we kept on walking through the clumps of people, the murmuring wash of noises, and the warm smells of sweat, sun and dust. They had to be around somewhere.

There! I pointed him out to Pretty-Girl. Down between the tipis walked a young warrior. His handsome face was turned away, but those thin shoulders had to belong to Shy-Bear. Oh, no, he led three of the ugliest horses ever stolen!

Pretty-Girl said nothing, just watched him attend to his mangy lot. Flies buzzed wearily over their bony shoulders. Each one had the dull brown coat of a travois-fitted mare. Packhorses! Shy-Bear must have taken them from the enemy's big herd at the edge of their camp, while the other young men had risked their necks by sneaking into camp to steal the more carefully guarded horses. What an old woman! I was as angry as Pretty-Girl should have been.

"Please do not say he is a coward, Sweetgrass. Please."

"How could your very own sweetheart do that to you? Go yell at him. He is standing right there, pretending he cannot hear a word."

"Hush, please. This is just the way it is." She watched quietly, head up and eyes wide as if testing the cold new wind on her life, while Shy-Bear walked away. "I would not want to maybe die either, just to steal horses."

"You are not a man!"

"Please do not be angry with him, Sweetgrass." That was all she could say.

Not be angry with him? Pretty-Girl would have to marry an old man now! Probably that creaky Five-Killer.

Oh, yes, some women marry worse men. But Pretty-Girl! It was so unfair! I wished I were a man. I wished I had power with Sun or the spirits, then I would stop this from happening. But there was nothing I could do.

There was certainly nothing I could say to Pretty-Girl,

who just stood there, eyes closed. I patted her on the arm and left her alone to do her own accepting. She could have my sympathy later, if she wanted it.

Perhaps Otter had gone home.

A new shouting began as I circled back the way we had come. Probably our band-chief was making a speech. Chiefs are always making speeches. One of our neighbors, ceremonially dressed in his beautiful blue trade-coat with all the lace, stood on my path home. His whole family was with him. One of the wives smiled over her shoulder at me, but no one moved to let me through.

Everyone seemed excited. What was it? I could not see over all those heads. I squirmed to the left, around the big belly of a very pregnant woman, and gasped in amazement.

Those two skinny boys smiling at me looked strangely familiar. Behind them my aunt Robe-Woman waved in greeting. Around her clustered some more of my uncle's wives and his twelve, no, sixteen children. Four more this year for Cuts-Both-Ways!

This then was the reason for the crowd's noise. My uncle's band had joined us here by the Red Deer River, a moon before we expected to meet them at the Sun Dance.

"Sweetgrass," my aunt cried, bustling forward from her place beside the band-chief, my uncle.

I waved in greeting. She was fatter than ever this year.

"How has Shabby-Bull, my brother, done this past winter? No problems with that gimpy leg of his? And Otter? And Bent-Over-Woman?"

I stammered a polite reply. My aunt's words trotted

on. . . . My eyes counted the new faces: somewhere in this crowd was my desire.

"Now, you will tell your almost-mother—oh, yes, and your grandmother too, as I expect she will have arrived at your tipi by now—all that I have told you about our campsite and also that—well, perhaps not, we will leave *that* for later. Still, in any event you are to tell her . . ." she continued.

"Sweetgrass," interrupted my older cousin Dog-Leg. "Will you tell Otter that you heard I stole a new racing pony? A beautiful gray, really fast. I bet anything I can beat him now!"

"Dog-Leg," his mother scolded. "Sweetgrass has too many messages to carry. Oh, yes, do not forget to tell my brother that your uncle Cuts-Both-Ways bought Favorite-Child a painted tipi design, a design of great power! I will describe it to him. There is your cousin, over there, wearing that new dress I made for her."

There Favorite-Child was indeed, quacking away at her almost-sisters and her friends. Some people feel *I'm* spoiled, but my cousin is the *minipoka*, the favorite child of all her powerful family, so she can quack as loud as she likes. Who ever looks down the throat of a beautiful woman?

"Sweetgrass!" Favorite-Child grinned and waved. "I will come and talk with you later."

Dog-Leg yelled back at her, "Poor Sweetgrass, you should promise to ignore her later!"

She made a bad face at him. I giggled.

"Do not tease your sister," said my aunt sternly. "Or your cousin."

My aunt made me repeat her instructions, then let me

leave. Going back to our tipi, I glimpsed the top of *his* head in the crowd! My heart leapt into my throat.

I noticed Favorite-Child was watching me over her shoulder, so I ducked behind an old man shrouded in wool blankets. There!

I glanced up the lean hard-muscled body to the puzzle of those laughing narrow eyes. Eagle-Sun! He must have been watching me.

I walked past him with my head modestly down, but each of my steps held a longing to dance. I wanted to stare back at him, but staring is not proper for a young woman.

His hair was tied with feathers. A quick look showed his shoulders grown even broader since last summer, the thin hard muscles standing out clearly beneath his brown skin.

Did I look as good to him?

That Eagle-Sun, he is a brave raider, the old men said. He is a fine hunter who brings home many buffalo. A generous, good-hearted young man, that one. Even my father agreed, but he added that no one should think of marriage so young. Bravery is for young men, wives are for old ones.

But Eagle-Sun already owned many horses. Would he soon ask for his childhood playfriend to be his wife?

The old people watched us. I should not stand near him. They all saw what I wanted and shook their heads. Wanting is not right for a young woman.

I lowered my eyes again and walked to our tipi. Grandmother would be there, my aunt had said. She winters with my aunt's family and she summers with us. Ever since she nursed Cuts-Both-Ways through a bad sickness six summers ago, they have been friends. But she still will not stay in his tipi, only in her own small one beside it. She lives in our tipi when she is with us. Father is Grandmother's only living son.

Grandmother is one person who cares about *me*. And right now Otter was probably having all of her attention to himself. The nuisance!

I had to talk to her. She could argue for me with Father. Maybe Father had already talked to her about when I would marry, and he tried to put her off. I will talk to her myself. I will fight! Grandmother understood fighters.

And Otter had better be waiting for me at the tipi.

"Grandmother!"

I found her sitting in the afternoon sun outside our tipi, her brown wrinkles calm in contemplation. Just looking at her gave me peace. Her small eyes, blue-black with age, peered up at me.

"So I see you again, my son's daughter," said She-Fought-Them-Woman. "Otter will greet you soon. He is in a boy's shame because the raiders only let him wait with their horses. I see you have been picking berries out on the hills."

"Strawberries, Grandmother." I opened a bag for her.

Stiffly her fingers moved to pincer a berry. Red leaked out, but it could not stain that skin hard-tanned by labor.

"They are good, Granddaughter." She reached for another.

"The strawberries taste sweeter this summer, I think."

"They have only tasted sweeter one summer that I remember, the summer that the smallpox came, long ago when I was a girl by the Missouri. But perhaps the berries taste good because they were picked by your young hands."

"My hands are not so young anymore. I am old for an unmarried woman."

Her face was calm, but her eyes were laughing. Why will no one take me seriously?

"Have my parents talked to you about my marriage?"

Her old eyes kept smiling. "It will happen soon enough. Do not worry."

"But what is a woman without a husband?"

"You ask me, a widow?" She rocked back and forth and laughed out loud. "A young woman should enjoy her time for dreaming, Sweetgrass. The time for a husband comes all too soon."

"But, Grandmother, I'm fifteen!"

"Most of a lifetime is time enough for men. You will find all they think about is buffalo and war. And they soon die—as did each of my husbands. Aiii, those were great warriors!"

Grandmother paused to choose another berry. "A Blackfoot woman lives only for her work and children. Enjoy yourself while you're young."

Old women do not remember what it is like to be young.

But it confused me that she would speak in that way. Grandmother herself had been a famous warrior. That was why they named her She-Fought-Them-Woman. With her first husband, she had ridden like the wind, stolen horses, and counted coup on the dead. Finally babies came and kept her near her tipi, but her story still was told. So how could she speak that way against warriors? And what did it have to do with me?

"Have you picked some sweetgrass to dry?" she calmly asked. I guessed she had seen the grass tucked in my hair.

"Not yet. Almost-Mother gives me too much work to do."

"Ah, you would rather pick strawberries than sweetgrass." She grinned with the lopsided face of the old. "Do remember that sweetgrass has the power of memories."

There, under her tight skin, I could see her skull. I shuddered. She moved and the outline was gone.

"Go into the tipi. Your grandmother wants to talk to her friends now. Bent-Over-Woman must have work for you to do, maybe even answers for all your questions."

I stepped inside the tipi to find Almost-Mother working in the dimmest light. She seemed to be counting empty food sacks. It was her duty to see that enough food was put away for each winter and she always started in the best days of summertime.

She frowned at me. "You are standing in the light."

I moved away from the tipi opening so that a thin sunfinger could shine toward her. Bits of dust swirled in the faint golden light. I wanted to marry and leave all this, leave her standing there, every line of her sagging downward.

"Almost-Mother, does Father seek a husband for me? Grandmother said I might ask you."

"She probably also said I would not tell you." Almost-

Mother's voice sounded high and flat, annoyed. "You will be told when we have chosen."

I squatted down, and started to help her with the sorting. The leather bags were cool in my hands. "Will you sew me a new dress, then?"

"What kind of a new dress? I do not have time to dye any porcupine quills."

"A dress embroidered with beads, then. To wear at the Sun Dance. Will you, Almost-Mother?"

She pinched her lips close together. "Sweetgrass, what are you asking?"

I waited for a moment, holding my stomach in tightly. She had stopped counting food sacks. When she looked back up at me her smile was sorry and she shook her head.

"Your father will tell you when it is time."

I tried pouting, but it didn't work.

"I want you to go over to your aunt Robe-Woman's campsite and help set up their tipi. And ask your aunt if she would like to pick saskatoons with us tomorrow. Their season is just starting."

"Yes, Almost-Mother."

"You and your cousin Favorite-Child could have a fine, long girltalk. My, it feels good to greet everyone again in the summer!"

Almost-Mother hummed a counting song under her breath and her hands returned to their work.

Perhaps I could see Eagle-Sun on the way, if luck was with me.

I squirmed through the tipi hole, my right leg first. Something hard hit the back of my knee, and down I went.

My head hurt and my hands hurt, but what really hurt was my pride. Especially when I heard my joke-playing brother Otter laughing as he ran away.

I pulled my skirt straight and wiped the dirt off my hands. I will never comb his hair free of his fellow vermin again! And I will certainly never worry about him and his stupid warpath either. He is only a man!

I hoped no one saw me fall.

Tomorrow morning I will have my revenge of Otter.

# 3

# REVENGE ON OTTER

WATER FLEW UP TO THE SUN. "SEE!" I CALLED OUT TO Favorite-Child as we thrashed the river in our morning swim. "The earth is crying with joy!"

Later on, the women of our family walked up the cliffs to the high plains where saskatoon bushes hung heavy with berries. Clear, glorious prairie light outlined the land around us. Somewhere in the upland the young men would be racing their horses. Otter had said so. My eyes strained to see them. I searched the skimming clouds for white peaks of mountains hidden in them, but we were still too far away. Soon, though, my people would see the mountains rising when we looked to the west.

Each day we would camp by a new patch of saskatoons. Slowly we moved west across the plains to our Sun Dance camp under the Belly Buttes, almost in the shadow of the mountains. The women would pick and dry berries for the winter while the men would talk and trade together, maybe smoke a bit. Later they might hunt a little.

At the Sun Dance, I would find my husband. I felt sure. My future was riding toward me, here as I waited.

How good it felt to be me! My blood sang strong beneath the sun. Favorite-Child was maybe prettier and wealthier than I was, but she couldn't flow with this hidden power. I felt mightier than a brave on the warpath. I felt I was holding the future like summer berries in my hands.

"So Pretty-Girl's father took horses for her at last," said Favorite-Child, breaking the silence.

"He did? Whose horses?"

"Five-Killer's. Yes, she is a little weak for a slavewife. That is sad," replied Favorite-Child. She pulled her handsome mouth down at the ends politely. "I am glad that I am going to be a first wife."

So she was glad. Favorite-Child had been promised to a famous warrior's son when she was just a baby. It was a fine match all right, but because the young man was a Piegan she had never seen him. And next year, when she was fifteen, she would go gladly to his tipi!

"I suppose we are lucky, you and me, for girls who live in such bad times," I answered.

"Bad times?" Favorite-Child narrowed her eyes at me.

"Such bad times, my grandmother always says." I tried to sound matter-of-fact, picking the purple berries steadily without even glancing at her.

A rustling noise interrupted me as someone pushed through the bushes. We looked up to see my almost-mother.

"What is wrong with you bad girls? Always lazy, always talking!"

"But, Almost-Mother . . ."

"You never notice when your mothers are leaving.

You stay and pick even the smallest berries, and leave none for the birds and animals! I pity the men you will marry."

Almost-Mother turned and walked stiff-leggedly away. Bent-Over-Woman always walked like she was tired. And the baby in the back-carrier made her look hump-backed. With graying hair sticking out from her braids like dirty feathers, she looked just like a crow.

"Your almost-mother is quick to get angry with you," said Favorite-Child. "Maybe my mother is being bossy-mean to her again."

Maybe. But I still do not like being cawed at. We gathered our bags and followed the old women.

They led us through some meadowlike prairie and then down to the bushy greenness bordering a thin and quiet stream.

Faint yelps of excitement blew to us on the breeze. Our mothers had led us nearer the horse racing! Close enough to hear, but not to see. Maybe at that very moment Eagle-Sun was racing one of his horses there.

These new saskatoon bushes shone darkly with ripe berries. We kneeled down and spread our blankets on the earth under them. When the berries grow this thick, it is quicker to beat them off with a stick. Then you just fill the berry bags from the blankets by hand-fuls.

"Almost-Mother is cross with me all the time," I continued where we left off. "That is part of what my grandmother means when she says these are bad times. You see, Father wanted to marry my mother, and she wanted to marry him. Mother was really old to get married, maybe eighteen, and he was only twenty-three. But they chose each other, and their parents thought it was good."

"No!"

"Yes. That was the way for many people, then. My parents chose each other. Later they took Mother's younger sisters to help with the work, but my father and my mother always felt chosen by each other."

I finished pulling the last blanket, even straightening a small fold in it where the cloth bulged over a root. Favorite-Child stood up too and we began to hit the berries off with our sticks.

But I had not finished saying what I wanted. "When I was not even a winter old, my mother's smallest sister died. Then my mother died the next winter having another baby who died too."

"Many women die that way. One of my sisters did."

"Yes. But that is why Father spoils me, so says my grandmother. And why Almost-Mother is so quick with me sometimes. Because my father and my mother had so much care for each other."

"That is strange. I hardly know anyone who marries that way now." Favorite-Child's mouth twisted up, then down. It looked like she wanted to believe it, but would not let herself. "You talk too much, Sweetgrass."

"Grandmother says it is bad times for women now, not so much for men. Back in the dog days when my grandmother's grandmother was a girl, that was a good time. Then sometime later we got horses from the south tribes and guns from the Cree in the north."

"But guns and horses are fine," exclaimed Favorite-

Child. "Aiii, we are the mighty Blackfoot! We have more horses and guns than anybody!"

"But Grandmother says . . ."

*"But Grandmother says . . ."*

I ignored her. "Grandmother says before men had guns they lived much longer. Most of our warriors did not die young. Men had fewer things to trade for, so women did not have to marry young to tan buffalo hides for trading. In the dog days, she says, most men took only one wife. . . ."

*"Kimataps,"* snorted Favorite-Child.

"No, not just poor men. Everybody. Men took only one wife and no more, because they were happy together. Grandmother says the price for a wife was lower, too. It was just a gift then, like a girl's gift is to the man's family now."

I whacked the red-purple berries savagely. "Back then, Pretty-Girl could have married Shy-Bear!"

I glanced sideways to see how my cousin was hearing this. The story was dreamy enough to make even the lucky Favorite-Child look faraway for a moment.

"I wish we had been born in the old times, Sweetgrass."

We stopped working for a while. I offered her berries from my bag and we sat down to eat. Maybe our mothers would be annoyed, but we were hungry. The main pemmican supplies would come from our fall-picked berries, not from this summer crop.

"Maybe it will work out for Pretty-Girl," I added. The berries made me feel full inside.

"Maybe," agreed Favorite-Child. "If Pretty-Girl is

loving and clever—and of course she will be loving and clever—she could be Chief Five-Killer's sits-beside-him wife, just as if she were the first married. Even today such things happen."

My mouth was sweet with agreement.

"You and I will have fine marriages," I began on a different tack. I wanted to talk about my dream. "You are going to marry a wealthy warrior, and share his tipi and his sacred medicine pipes. Together with him you will greet your guests. Later you will become a Sun Dance woman, and your virtue and dignity will be known to everyone. And your husband will honor you. You will see. I am going to marry a man who is young, and kind, and handsome, and—"

"But the man you like has a big beak of a nose. That is not handsome!" giggled Favorite-Child.

I ignored her.

"And handsome! With a *handsome* nose! And he will like me. He will not *ever* tire of me and want more wives. Perhaps he will even stay home from the warpath when we are married. Such things have happened . . . for a year or two. You and me, we will have fine lives!"

The sun, the sky, the breeze that touched my cheek felt like a promise of happiness. Sunshine hung around me like a warm blanket, softer than the finest buckskin.

Then a high sound rose joyfully into the sky, echoing the day's promise. A song, a warrior song! And hoof-beats! The young men were coming.

A gray horse, a black, and a white-starred bay came galloping with laughing riders. They charged toward us over the meadow, through the tall grass and green poplar saplings, and those that did not bend aside got trampled. Favorite-Child and I laughed with delight at the young men in their ride of power.

I saw Favorite-Child's brother, Dog-Leg, and behind him Otter, the youngest of them all. My almost-brother was the only boy who could ride with the young men. Otter made his stallion dance on its hind legs for us. Favorite-Child laughed. I was proud. His riding was so good that Father promised him a man's place when we came to the fall hunting.

Safe behind bushes, I threw a handful of berries at Otter. He just laughed and ducked them.

At the end of the group rode Eagle-Sun.

His skin was tanned red-brown, the deep red-brown that is the color of buffalo-calf fur in the autumn. Slim with rope-tight muscles, he rode his horse bareback. A light seemed to shine in his eyes, and there was a hint of a smile at the ends of his long, thin mouth as he looked down at me. Favorite-Child threw more berries and kept screaming with laughter, even at Eagle-Sun. But I did not dare.

I was silent and watched him. He was silent and watched me. Oh, Father, let me marry him!

Finally my sweetheart rode back to the meadow to where the others were waiting. Otter leaped off his horse and took a ball out of his saddlebag. The young men were going to play a game to show off for us.

We turned back to our bushes but continued to watch the young men. Their happy voices kept us company. Deep among them was my sweetheart's.

"Sweetgrass! Sweeeetgrass!" My aunt waddled toward

us, panting from the heat. Her buckskin underclothes must have been sticking together. Obviously, she was coming with a job for me.

"Aiii, look at your bags, girls! Still so many empty? You must be eating berries." Then she smiled at my cousin. "But it is hard for the young not to indulge, and they do smell good, hot from the sun." Now she stopped smiling. "Sweetgrass, I have an errand for you."

My aunt would never send Favorite-Child.

"As we are going to be late back to camp and the boys will get there much faster, I want you to go tell my almost-son Dog-Leg to tell his mother that Father is feasting tonight. My husband asked several great warriors to come and smoke with him. So the younger wives must start making fine dishes of food now. I will be in time to set it before the men. That is all."

The high meadow was a good place to walk. The sun beat down and a breeze kept me cool. I drove a grasshopper in front of me for a while. Step just behind him: chirrr, step, chirrr, step.

Finally he found a safer trail of his own. Then I came across a puffball, looking like a smooth, white throwing-size stone, and picked it up. Too bad it was light in my hand. Its tasty insides had ripened to powder. An idea jumped into my mind, so I did not throw it away.

Dog-Leg stood by a clump of trees watching a foot race. He turned his kind brown eyes to me as I came near him.

"I bet you have a message from my almost-mother." He sure knew Robe-Woman.

But before I could reply, a rosebush slapped me across

the back of the head, stinging me where my hair parted. This time I forced my body to relax, then quietly turned to look at the troublemaker behind me.

"Hello, Otter," I said with a calm face that I knew would disappoint him. "I was sent to give Dog-Leg a message, but I also have one for you."

I spent more time than I should have telling Dog-Leg about his father's feast and the message he was to carry back, but I wanted to get Otter wondering.

Then I turned on my heel and started back across the meadow with dignity. Otter scampered behind, the way I knew he would.

"What was my message? Was there no message for me?" he yapped.

But I just kept walking.

"A sister is supposed to have respect for her brother. Stop and give me the message."

He danced around in front of me, blocking my path with outstretched arms. So I held my fist, curled around the dry puffball, to my chin, and frowned as if I had forgotten.

"I was supposed to give you . . ."

"Come on, you fly-memory!"

Then I brightened up like I remembered. I glanced around like it was a very *secret* message and leaned closer.

"Yes, yes?" he stepped closer. Closer.

"I was supposed to give you . . ." I whispered, then mushed the puffball into his face ". . . a taste of your own medicine!"

I leaped sideways and raced away through the grass.

By this time, all the young men had stopped their games and were laughing and pointing.

He chased me, wiping the powder from his eyes. "You sneak, you stung me!"

"What is a sting to the noble Otter?" I shouted back as loudly as I could. "How could *anything* hurt a mighty warrior who makes such brave ambushes on his sister?"

"You mangy gopher!"

We were getting quite close to the women's berry bushes. Hopefully they could hear us.

"You rotten, dog-faced mongrel!" He was furious.

Almost-Mother stepped out from behind a bush and grabbed Otter by the ear. "Such dreadful names!"

Oh, this was too good!

"You should always be kind to your almost-sister," she scolded. Perhaps Otter might leave me alone for a while now.

Across the meadow I could hear Eagle-Sun's deep laughter. Would my brother ever be teased when he skulked back to his friends!

My almost-mother had words for me too.

"Sweetgrass," she scolded, "what a thing for a young woman to do! It will shame me to tell your father. How can we send you in marriage when you behave like this?"

She rumbled off toward camp. I followed with my head lowered obediently, my spirits unrepentant. Behind me, Favorite-Child giggled, but my ears heard only another's laughter.

At least I had shown myself no coward.

I had, had I not?

# 4

# THE RIVER OMEN

NEXT DAY, WHEN THE SUN ROSE, MY FRIEND PRETTY-
Girl went to the tipi of her husband. She took with her
the usual dowry of dried meat and moccasins, blankets
and backrests—-but no horses for carrying her things
when camp moved. That was all right. Five-Killer had
enough horses already.

I heard the busy noises in that side of camp, but I did
not go to watch. I did not want to see her. Maybe Pretty-
Girl was nervous about going to Five-Killer's tipi. Maybe
she did not want her friends there either.

Besides, we had agreed to get up in the gray dawn after
two nights passed and haul water from the river together.
Then the two of us would be alone to talk.

A dim light filtered down through the open smokehole
of our tipi. My eyes saw that it was time to get up and my
mind knew it as well, but my body still swam in the cool
water of sleep. How to capture myself?

There was a tickling in my toes, so I stretched them
first and then the muscles in my feet and ankles. Pushing

my scratchy Hudson's Bay blankets aside, I rose into the dawning. On the other side of camp Pretty-Girl would be slipping away from her bed too . . . but by her bed, there would lie a husband.

What would she tell me by the silence of the river?

I pulled our tipi flap open and swung out into a strange gray world. Mist had stolen into my people's camp, and it held us all surrounded. I listened, and heard nothing. No mothers rising, relighting the tipi fires. No fathers leading young boys down to the morning river.

But a little quiet was not going to frighten me. What could go wrong? This was my best friend's first day in marriage.

The bladderskins bumped against my legs as I padded across our campsite. Last night I dreamt Eagle-Sun asked for me in marriage. I had to tell someone. Ah, there at the camp's edge stood Pretty-Girl, waiting and yawning.

Her eyes widened in greeting. We ran to meet each other.

Aiii! What was that? The first loud sound of the day snarled from the tipi nearest us, Mane-Like-Fox's tipi.

His fat wife was snoring! Pretty-Girl and I tottered toward the bank of the river, holding each other's arms to ease our laughter.

"A snore like a buffalo snort," I gasped. And we clutched our stomachs. We must not wake the camp.

Pretty-Girl was laughing more than usual. Marriage must make her happy.

Down among the soft spikes of rushes, no one but us bent over the river. Not even one bird flew near. The dawning day lay wrapped in mystery, and we were alone. This mist, this grayness, this quiet demanded dignity.

"Pretty-Girl?" I whispered.

"Yes?" She was bending silent now, filling her water bags.

"How does it feel, being married?"

"Aiii, you *know* what it feels like, Sweetgrass. It feels like being one of all the other married women."

The river air was sharp and smelled of other times and places. Dark shapes slipped through the green river water. I watched a big one slowly moving.

"What is it like for you?"

"I told you."

"But do you feel different? Do you like it? How is it different from living in your parents' tipi?"

Pretty-Girl looked down at the river. "I have bigger water bags to carry."

"You have always carried big ones. You carry more than my almost-mother does. How does it *feel* to you?" I scratched at some mud on my water bag. If you don't look at someone when you ask them a delicate question, their answer sometimes comes more easily.

"Five-Killer tells me what to do just like Father. The oldest wife, she is just like Mother."

Her dark eyes were secret, wet like the river. I guessed she had stopped worrying about Shy-Bear. But why did she not tell me how it feels *being someone married?*

I filled my last water bag. Light began to flicker over the rippling shapes in the water. They lapped green, then blue, then clear when the cold wind let up for a breath. One moment of calm flowed over a large

dark shape on the river bottom, revealing a great fish—
one of the mysterious water people, one of the river
spirits.

I threw a stone at it and it was away.

I shivered. Maybe my friend needed to be cheered up.
"Pretty-Girl, do any of Five-Killer's older wives snore like
buffalo?"

Pretty-Girl laughed. "No, but he does!"

"Does it make you unhappy?"

"No, but nobody gets married to be happy."

"I am going to marry and be happy."

"Perhaps, but you have got to marry because it is the
only thing a Blackfoot woman can do. My father wanted
a son-in-law. He needed help."

"But your father never made you marry, did he?"

"No, but he did not let me choose either. And I am
not going to go shooting my own buffalo, after all!"
Then Pretty-Girl spit it out. "I *had* to marry!"

"You will like some parts of being married."

"Five-Killer will give me children."

"Oh, I am sure he will give you other fine things."

"He will just give me children."

This was not right. I knew married women who
were happy and respected, honored women who sponsored Sun Dances and had visions. Their sons came
with fine gifts. Their men asked for help in advice and
healing.

But now the reeds, the silence, the mist over the water
somehow grew on me as blindly threatening.

Or was I only feeling it more since we stopped talking?
Pretty-Girl started listening too now.

"There is something wrong here," she said.

Yes, it was still the gray dawn, still the dangerous time. I listened hard but could hear only my heartbeat.

There was nothing else my ears could find a name for. We looked at each other in dread wonder.

Pretty-Girl bent down first, then I did, to lift the skins we had filled with water. We scrambled up the grass banks, caring little about knees scratched or smeared with river clay. The silence was not only ourselves. We stumbled faster and faster. Finally I was half running with my water bags sloshing over. Water ran trickling down my legs. My soaked moccasins twisted against me at every breathless step.

And still there was no sound behind us.

We ran on, not knowing why. The mist was lifting as we ran, but that brought no answers. Landmarks stayed both dim and unsafe, as if some mystery lurked behind the stones and the alder bushes.

What evil had we heard or felt, beyond this too-deep silence?

I searched my mind for memories of earlier disasters. There had been enemy horse raids. No, wrong feeling. A buffalo herd stampeded and flattened our camp, but the sound was what frightened me then.

This was something quiet.

Two eyes set in fur stared from a hole as we raced by. I remembered the wounded she-bear that had smashed her way through our foothills camp one winter. But this time the fear felt . . . larger. The danger-force felt big, or many, or spread out.

What was the sign?

It certainly was not some young Cree or Crow hiding in the rushes, wanting to make love to us.

Pretty-Girl hurried ahead of me over the short grasses.

"Why are we running?" I cried.

Her face turned halfway back, and I was slapped again with fear. She didn't see me, only terror. What if she dropped her water bags?

The ache in my belly deepened. I had to help that girl.

I ran closer, grabbing the trailing strings of one water bag, and tugged, but she did not let go. Did she not know I was trying to help?

"Let me . . . carry one of . . . your bags," I panted.

"No."

"I am older."

"I am married."

"Listen . . . see . . . your bags . . . spilling over us. Too wet to run . . . soon." She let me take a bag from her then, no protests.

My shoulders burned with the weight of the bags; it felt like my arms were ripping out of my body. The last bend in the trail. My right hand, tight around two sets of bag strings, numbly began to open. It did not feel like mine anymore. Were those gray shapes the tipis? I ran and ran though I did not know why.

As our camp loomed through the last clinging feathers of mist, the bag straps slid again. Now they were just hanging on the tips of my dead fingers. Please do not slip. If I lost my water, I could not possibly make myself go back to the river.

Then we were inside the safe circle of tipis. Mane-Like-Fox's fat wife was still snoring cheerfully.

I rested my bags on the soft earth beside me. I was a calf safe in my own herd of buffalo. Pretty-Girl pulled off her bag strings, too, but neither of us looked at the other. We each went our own wet way home, with few words of parting and no backward glances.

How would Pretty-Girl explain to Five-Killer why her long hair was sweat-sleek as mink fur? How would she explain to Five-Killer's Sits-Beside-Him wife the thinness of her water bags? If sent back to the river would she, like me, refuse to go?

If I were a warrior, I could gather friends to hunt game by the river. Then we would either see my signs again or not. A warrior can move with dignity against his fears. But there was nothing I could do.

I could come back crying and begging them to save me from a danger that might be alive and near. Otter would then laugh at me and Father would say I was not old enough for marriage.

What would make them take me seriously? I flipped my braids back, pulled my shoulders straight and tried to smooth my steps into grace and dignity.

My grandmother was squatting outside our tipi, arranging dry grass over old buffalo chips so they would take light quickly.

"Sweetgrass?" she said, dropping her firesteel at the sight of me. Then she smiled and picked it up and hit it against her flint for the spark to start our fire. Grandmother knows how to right her wrongs. Maybe I could be that way.

I calmly opened our tipi flap and swung myself in, catching my right foot and making the poles shake. Aiii.

"Almost-Daughter? Is that you?" Bent-Over-Woman called, peering out from her night nest of furs.

"Yes, Almost-Mother. Pretty-Girl and I went down to the river."

"Down to the river looking for lovers, I bet," murmured Otter sleepily through the hair that covered his face and his weasel eyes. I wanted to empty a water bag over his lazy head.

Would they laugh at me for a little girl if I told them about the river silence? What if something bad came and I had said nothing? The thought squirmed in my belly.

But I was afraid to look afraid.

Grandmother would say if I kept my mouth shut when I should speak, a great flood of pain might wash over the camp—all because of my small fear for myself. So I said, "There is something strange, maybe, down by the river."

Then I emptied a bladderskin bag of water defiantly into the hush so they could not laugh. The water splashing against the black kettle bottom kept everyone quiet. The last water dripped slowly from the bag's rim. Three drops, one drop, then none. No one yet spoke to me.

Almost-Mother finally pushed off her blankets and sat up. She combed her hair slowly and grumbled, but it was only her usual morning grumble. Father lay silent, his blanket pulled up to cover his nose. Ignoring them back was easy in the tipi's half-darkness.

Outside in that fog waited something I had forgotten, my other water bag dropped by the flap in my hurry.

Reluctantly I padded across the floor to get it. My left foot lifted over the door flap. My right foot . . .

Aiii! I could not move my right foot. I looked down to see my father's big hand gripping my ankle.

"Be quiet," he growled softly.

We held still as the cold stone of the mountains.

Faint high screams of alarm were rising from Five-Killer's side of camp. That was why my father listened. We were under attack!

# 5

# ATTACKED!

OUR BABY CRIED. SHE HOWLED AND HOWLED AS SHE never had before. Blackfoot babies must always be quiet: death can follow careless noise so easily. What if an enemy warrior heard the baby?

With Father and Otter gone, blown out on the blood-scented wind of morning, we were left alone. I listened fearfully at the door flap for the sound of footsteps. Killing women and children is the easiest way to count coup.

Grandmother prowled around our tipi, hunting with the growing light for weapons our men might have left behind. Almost-Mother crouched in the darkness under the farthest slope, trying to force her breast into the mouth of the howling treacherous baby. I listened to men yell and horses scream as the battle welled up around us.

Inside, our baby spluttered and choked. The rest of us waited in silence. I didn't even talk when Little-Brother toddled over to me. He shoved his soft, small face into the hollow behind my knees and clung there. The feathery touch on my skin was his blinking eyelashes. Awkwardly, I stood listening, afraid to move.

If I were a man, I could charge into battle. But I was a girl—my job was to avoid it, and get us all through to safety. The strange war cries, sounding again and again, got nearer. Had Grandmother found any weapons?

Slowly our baby's cries died down to gentle sobbing. Maybe she would soon accept Almost-Mother's breast. But the sound of the crying was not quite right to me.

I listened, weighing the sound. Someone was crying along with our baby.

Almost-Mother's face was turned away from me, but I could see her shoulders shaking just a little. All of her was curled around the body of our baby. Weak protection, but part of me wanted to huddle with them. What else could we do except hide ourselves? When Almost-Mother moaned under her breath, I felt a snaky uneasiness stir inside me. Old war stories flooded into memory.

In a long-ago attack, a woman of my band was killed by a knife thrust through her tipi's wall. My own uncle died from an arrow that came the same way.

So I gave Little-Brother a quick hug, and sat him down whimpering in the center of the tipi floor. I ignored him and crossed over to my almost-mother's side.

"Are you hurt, Almost-Mother?"

Sweat dripped from her forehead onto the baby. She did not seem to notice when I touched her graying hair.

"Almost-Mother?"

There was no blood anywhere.

"Grandmother?" My whisper begged her to tell me what to do, but she was busy turning a long ceremonial lance around in her hands, thoughtfully testing its weight.

"Grandmother, what is wrong with Almost-Mother?"

Dignity and sore old bones slowed her walk, but she came and looked. "All things are well here."

But Almost-Mother did not look well at all.

"Come and look at these weapons, Sweetgrass," Grandmother said. "There is no hurt on that one."

"Then why is she crying?"

Grandmother looked at me. Her eyes seemed very small. Then she spoke right through me to Almost-Mother as if I were not there.

"Stand now, Wife-of-My-Son!"

"I am afraid, Husband's-Mother."

"You will die in your fear," the old woman scolded in a harsh whisper. "Stand and save your children. Be strong and mighty like a true Blackfoot."

Grandmother beckoned to me with her clawed fingers. I tried to smile at Almost-Mother, but followed the older woman.

"But Grandmother, what can we do except cry?"

Grandmother snorted. "We are not waiting for others to decide our fate! Open the tipi flap a little and tell me what you see with your young eyes."

I looked at the tied flap.

"Perhaps it is only a big horse-stealing raid," my grandmother said, more gently. "Perhaps our warriors have the enemy on the run."

"But if it is a real attack?"

"Then the enemy may be hiding in the long grass on the edge of camp. You will see arrows fly, hear the guns shoot."

WHACK! That musket ball was no less than the length of a dead dog away.

Did Grandmother expect me to look outside at that?

Whatever was happening? I listened inside myself for a sign, but found only humming darkness. I watched the edges of my sight for flickering spirits, but saw nothing, nothing at all.

I could not bring myself to open the flap. Grandmother frowned impatiently. I had to face the battle.

I pulled the smallest corner of the flap back, just far enough for one of my eyes. If an arrow found me I would only be half-blinded. A child's thought! I must think mighty woman thoughts. I must!

My grandmother, she was a lifelong stubborn woman. Me, I wanted to die quickly, not in little bits struggling for handholds.

"Sweetgrass!" growled Grandmother.

I flipped a small corner of the flap back, did a fast peep and closed it up again. Outside looked brown, not the grassy green that should lie between us and the next tipi. What did I see? A dead thing? My mind gave over to many pictures of that. Maybe it was a horse ground-rolled with his legs in the air and flies crawling all over him. Or an eagle-feathered enemy warrior, his stiff arm pointing at me, guiding his friends to their revenge.

"What do you see?" said Grandmother.

Fearful things.

I forced my eye back to the hole and saw the fuzzy brown again. It was just dark river-edge dirt. The horses' hooves must have kicked off the grass covering.

And there were no dead ones. That was a good sign, but my stomach twisted inside with shame.

Without moving, I looked all around. Nothing looked

very strange except for more dirt patches here and there, and the clumps of torn grass.

I raised myself a little to look down the side of our tipi. There my lost water bag waited for rescue. What a sad little headless animal! An arrow could splatter it right open.

I threw the flap back and stepped out to lift it to safety. Here was something proper to do. Practical, my almost-mother would say. I slung it into the tipi without losing a drop, then straightened up and glanced around.

My foolishness hit me full force. An arrow, lance or bullet could easily have smashed me first. I had stepped into a battleground without even a broad-angled look!

I moved fast, back tight against the tipi, sucking my shadow into thin shade. My heart pounded. No warriors hiding in the long grass under the trees. No warriors creeping between the tipis with guns in their hands. I saw no horses and I saw no men. The noise of rifles and muskets seemed not so rib-cracking close. Smoke rose over Five-Killer's side of camp. Had the fighting moved back there? Maybe our enemies were being driven away.

I swung myself inside to tell the others. Grandmother smiled at my courage. "What should we do next?" I whispered to her.

"No one in the long grass?"

"I saw, felt no one."

"No guns?"

"No guns here, only on Five-Killer's side. Maybe it was a horse raid that went wrong, and our men surprised them." I looked down at my twisting hands, slippery with sweat. When did that happen?

My grandmother seemed to be counting something inside her head. Her closed eyelids fluttered softly, like feathers falling in uncertain air. Finally she said, "Those war cries are Assiniboin."

"Aiii."

"Their warriors shoot through tipis and burn them. I can feel them. Too near, very angry. We must leave, *now*. You pack what I say and I will change the baby."

Grandmother listed off water, dried food, moccasins, our firesteel, flint and weapons. The trees outside camp, she said, would hide us until the fight was over. If the worst happened, we could even cross the prairie till we found some other Blackfoot camp and there ask for refuge.

Speaking calmly and deliberately, Grandmother undid the laces of the baby's carrying bag. The baby made a face at her own bad stink. She really needed her moss changed.

Little-Brother watched wide-eyed as Grandmother dumped the moss onto the hide floor of our tipi. It was the right thing to do under the circumstances. Our baby smiled and kicked as Grandmother packed clean, dry moss around her bottom.

"Sweetgrass, you will walk first and lead the others." She put the papoose on my back. "You will also carry the weapon."

A ceremonial lance. I had never learned how to use one!

"And I will carry Little-Brother." Grandmother smiled at him as if nothing were wrong. He would slow us down otherwise. His big sad eyes followed my every move as I finished putting together his mother's pack.

I forced my lips to give him a brave smile.

Little-Brother grinned back shyly and disappeared down into his warm sleeping-robes.

My hands moved swiftly between the bags, scooping pemmican from large into smaller, more packable skins. "Almost-Mother, could you pass me the moccasin bag?"

"Oh, we will be slaves of the Assiniboin," she wailed, staring at me stupidly, "or maybe even killed."

The crackling of the gunfire had come around again. If only we were men, knowing how the battle went, knowing how to change it!

"We will not be taken, Almost-Mother." My mouth was dry. I tried to swallow, but the bitter gunpowder taste stuck in my throat. "We will not be taken."

She was sobbing openly now.

"We will be safe in the woods," I said as surely as I could, but she was having none of that. "Please move over so I can reach the moccasin bag."

Almost-Mother moaned loudly.

My grandmother padded softly over to us. "Aiii, Wife-of-My-Son," she said, "now you must prove yourself a fine Blackfoot. You will carry our water and our pemmican and our extra moccasins."

I helped Grandmother load Almost-Mother, which was the last thing to be done before we left. We tied each thing on her as we would a packhorse. I even had to check her straps to make sure nothing would rub or cut her skin. She just stood there, muttering about waiting for Shabby-Bull and Otter.

"You speak of our warriors," said Grandmother as she packed. "I have myself been a warrior. Their lives without our lives are worth less than our lives without theirs.

· 53 ·

We Blackfoot women must expect our men to die at any moment, and we must be strong to do our part. We are to save our lives and the lives of our Blackfoot children."

Grandmother turned to me. "Do you remember the song that warriors sing before they go on the warpath?"

I nodded.

"Do you also remember the Going-Away-Song, Bent-Over-Woman?"

"Yes, I remember, Husband's-Mother."

"The warriors sing, 'We go, but the women shall still bear children. Our tribe shall never end.'"

Grandmother seemed pleased to see Almost-Mother gathering her spirits.

"Now be mighty Blackfoot women and take up your loads."

Pushing my arms through the cradleboard straps, I bent my back under the weight of our baby. She was asleep at last. I made a quick prayer that she stay that way for a long time. Last of all, I picked up the ceremonial lance. What would it feel like killing food with it? Or, for that matter, spearing an enemy warrior?

The old woman gathered up Little-Brother and led us out of the tipi.

Dust was swirling everywhere. Horses and warriors dashed in and out of the clouds like dream figures. We set to crawling a narrow line of peace between the clash and the cries, hiding on the quiet side of each tipi as we came to it.

Dust gritted between my tongue and teeth. I gathered my strength into my lance hand and promised myself I would thrust fiercely into anyone who stopped us. Just let him dare!

We dragged on our bellies like snakes, closer and closer to the sheltering poplars. They were fine trees to see, but would we ever be amongst them?

The covering of the last tipi felt warm against my side. It would be hard to leave. My turn first. If I made it across, I was to wave the others over when it was safe. Almost-Mother was next, then Grandmother.

The open ground stretched before me with no place to hide. Who might see me when I ran across? I felt a little sick when I crouched close to the earth. Then, head down, I ran.

I remember every footprint, every stone I ran over. I remember the height of the sun, a hand's breadth above the tipi tops. I remember the grass blades underfoot as I heard the thunder coming down halfway across the big field. Aiii! From that big thunder to the left, one small thunder came apart and drove directly at me. A horse's hooves, a deep rumbling clatter. My feet threw clumps and clumps of space behind me.

The forest grasses clung trembling to my body. Trees whipped above me as I swam through their thick undergrowth, pushing desperately.

A huge, black shape loomed up on my left. Glaring eyes. Assiniboin warrior's pointed topknot. Gun's eye. Was it looking at me?

On and on I ran, shadow looming over me. My mind raced too. Around and around, over and over. I, with no power, what can I do? Sun, anyone, I will promise! The gun's eye stared steadily. Save me!

I watched my legs as they ran in slow motion. Then, BANG, a giant hand hit my shoulder and pushed me nose-deep into the dirt.

There was dust in my mouth for real now. Blackness filled my eyes. Was I alive? My shoulder hurt, hurt bad.

The baby cried high and thin on my back. There were growly voices too. Someone fumbled with the baby's straps and lifted her off me. Give her back, I shouted in my mind, but had no breath to say it.

Her cries got lost in the buzz of voices nearby. I had done it wrong, all wrong. My shoulder burned fiery-hot against the cool ground, and I could not make its fire go out.

Someone touched my arm, and I moaned.

"It is I, Sweetgrass," said a deep voice at my side. Father! "Do not be afraid for the little one. She is safe," he said, hugging the baby.

"My shoulder hurts, Father."

"If it hurts, you are alive."

The other voices laughed with him. Did I look funny in the dirt? Many hands turned me over and someone asked, "Shabby-Bull, did your daughter let that dirty Assiniboin escape?" This brought down more laughter. They were all my own people, but I would not look.

Father touched my sore arm again. "It is only a scratch, Sweetgrass. Not deep. You are lucky."

I hurt.

"Open your eyes and dust off your clothes. How can a daughter of my family whimper so much?"

I could hear him and the cruel laughter of the people behind him. I opened my eyes, shook my head and the pain stepped back. I felt my strength straightening inside of me. I would not be laughed at.

"Good girl!"

Dignity helped smooth my face. The people all

stopped looking at me and fell to talking to each other. I sat up and looked around. Favorite-Child was there, but not Pretty-Girl . . . and where was Eagle-Sun?

"Was anyone . . . ?"

"No one was killed, daughter. One of the young warriors—that Shy-Bear—took a musket ball in his side. The healer woman will mend him." Father lifted his head to smile at Grandmother as she joined us. "Well, Mother, is my daughter fierce? Or is she a coward?"

"A coward? No, my little Sobbing-in-the-Night." I noticed she called Father by his childhood name. "Sweetgrass will be a warrior woman."

A warrior woman? Me?

"This bad puppy?"

With quick short strokes she beat the dust from my hair. Tugging the left braid, she leaned close and grinned. "And such a strong one!"

She turned back to Father and told him everything we had done during the raid. She described in detail how fearlessly I had gone out of the tipi to scout around, how I had remained calm and helped pack up, how I led the escape.

It was not exactly like that, but I was pleased to see Father nod and smile. Thank you, Grandmother!

After the healer woman had seen to Shy-Bear, she came to bandage my sore shoulder. It would feel good soon, she said, but I was hard-pressed to keep my face calm when she washed out the dirt. All afternoon and all night my shoulder ached. And the loud speeches kept sleep away.

The old men held a council that night to discuss the

Assiniboin attack. They passed the pipe around many times. Maybe the enemy would return with more warriors. Maybe we should strike back first. Maybe . . .

In the end, the council decided to move camp early. That pleased Grandmother, and in the morning she told me why.

"The time has come to move toward the Sun Dance. We must not be late getting to our campsite under the Belly Buttes. The Berry Moon is ripening fast."

"The time has come," agreed Otter. "Berries have become purple, and the buffalo cover the hills like one great robe for Sun. The old men should go check their day-counts."

Otter often spoke like that now, like he was an old man already. Sometimes it was hard to take. But he *had* been given a vision of himself killing his own buffalo. His spirit helper said that Otter would become a man soon, maybe get a new name next summer. My brother's eyes burned with hope, and he was only at the peak of his twelfth summer.

And I was already fifteen. As I folded our tipi cover and helped Almost-Mother load it onto the horse's travois, my mind kept returning to the same question. Do they consider me woman enough to be married?

# 6

## SUN DANCE

Even the dust of our Sun Dance camp was lively. It rose, stirred by naked dancing children and scruffy yellow dogs snapping at their heels. All things seemed to travel up to the sky—smoke, dust and noise. My heart rose as I watched.

Chief Mountain, *Ninastako,* looked down from on high at this busy hive.

Everyone was at the Sun Dance, the great yearly gathering of our tribe for religious ceremonies—and to enjoy each other! All my cousins were there, all my aunts and uncles, and my old friends I had not seen since our last Sun Dance. There were many famous people to watch for, also. All the celebrated healers and all the past Sun Dance Women could be seen in their best clothes and facepaint. Many a great chief or a powerful *na-tose,* man of power, walked the camp.

Here our great men displayed their new trade goods. There were many fine English things from the Hudson's Bay Company, north at Fort Edmonton, or different goods from the American trading posts south at forts

McKenzie and Union. My aunt Robe-Woman had a new metal ring, very nice.

My uncle Cuts-Both-Ways had many new goods, too. As he had given away so many fine gifts this year, everyone said he was a wealthy man. He had distributed blankets to several *kimataps* families in his own band and to some of his own poor relatives in others. A chief who is generous as well as wise makes life as sweet as honey.

The hustle and the bustle reminded me of last summer when Pretty-Girl and I had walked through these crowds together. We stared at my uncle's lace shirt from the American traders. It was white then, a very fine shirt, with ruffles on its front and sleeves.

We had dodged those men who were loud with American whiskey, and giggled behind their backs.

The best part was to have a young warrior catch your eye. If you looked back, you were flirting.

But that was last year. This year the main Sun Dance pole soared into the sky as tall as ever, and the western mountains still stood over us like a council of old warriors. The crowds were just as big, the young men just as good to look at—but this year nothing felt the same. I had no one to walk with. Pretty-Girl had to clean her husband's buffalo hides all day at his tipi.

Chief Five-Killer was a mighty hunter, owning the finest guns and the best buffalo horses in camp, and his many young relatives owed him gifts of hides, as well. He was always generous with the young men; they gave things back to him double. But only his sits-beside-him wife had time free for gossiping.

The Sun Dance was a time for visiting and ceremonies, but not at Five-Killer's tipi.

I would have to see the camp's sights alone, without Pretty-Girl's cheerful voice beside me. It would have to be later, though. On this, the first morning of the first Sun Dance day, I also had to stay at home. My almost-mother gave me six great bags of dried berries to be pounded for pemmican. After that, I would have time to look at the young men. All she ever thought about was working.

I pounded the berries into a fine powder. At first it was not an unpleasant job. The mortar bowl was an old gray stone one, cool and smooth in my hands. I pounded until dust the color of dried blood filled the bowl.

The sun rose higher into the Sun Dance sky.

Old women came that morning to visit Grandmother. Father strolled off to visit with his friends, not even once looking at me work. Otter and Almost-Mother dipped in and out of the tipi all morning. No one stopped to talk with me.

Not only did I get lonely, but my knees felt like they were growing roots, and my arms, wrists and back tingled with the pounding. My half-healed shoulder began to hurt again. Still, no one stopped to talk.

Did no one in the whole camp feel friendly today? Several bags of Almost-Mother's berries still sat there, unground. I sighed as I poured more of them into the mortar.

When morning was half gone someone did come. At last! My cousin Favorite-Child came pulling one of her younger brothers by his dirty paw. He was yelling his head off. The boy still had his baby-round cheeks, but I guess he felt too old to be dragged around like that.

"Look at him!" Favorite-Child panted to me as they came up. "He cannot even sit on a horse yet, but he thinks he is a grown man!"

"I am a man!" he sobbed. "And you cannot force me to do things! You are a girl." He twisted and squirmed and whined while Favorite-Child held his wrists together.

When he flashed his dark, biting eyes at me, I had to laugh. "Where are you taking the little bull-calf?"

"Not a bull-calf!"

"Be polite, you bad puppy. I'm taking him to my father's parents. They are so lonely without children. He will play at their tipi for a few days and make them laugh," said Favorite-Child.

I looked at the wriggling little beast again. "Are you sure they can handle him?"

"Oh, he will be good at his grandparents'. He just doesn't want to be *taken* there. By a *girl!*"

When she dragged out the word just like he did, I couldn't help but laugh.

"You will still be here when I come back?"

"I have to pound these berries."

"Then we can talk."

I felt much happier.

As she dragged off her little brother, Favorite-Child fluttered her eyelashes over her shoulders. "Aiii! I forgot. I have something special to tell you. . . ."

My stomach jumped. "Tell me now, Favorite-Child."

But my cousin's face twisted suddenly. Little-Brother had twisted himself around to sink his teeth into his sister's fine brown arm. The two of them struggled off, yapping like coyote pups.

I poured out more berries and wondered what her secret could be.

Maybe I already knew. Two tipis from ours to the east, there was a tipi circled with red dots all the way around. It was a special design, and I knew who carried the right to those puffballs: White-Crow and his sits-beside-him wife, Laughing-Woman, parents of Eagle-Sun!

They had chosen to set their tipi up near ours. Now I could see him come and go. I could even talk with him . . . if he wanted to talk with me.

There were many other handsome young men if Eagle-Sun did not want me. Maybe he would see us talking and then want me.

Our tipis could have been set up like this for a special reason. Maybe our parents wanted to speak about promising me to him, even about letting us have our own tipi this very Sun Dance! They might do that. I pounded my almost-mother's berries with new interest.

A few berries sweeten much pemmican if they are ground fine like ashes. I pounded them over and over. The only problem was, it was hard to pour them into the pemmican bags while watching the door of the spotted tipi.

I felt sure someone would come out. Finally someone did, but it was not Eagle-Sun—only his mother. Would she come and talk to me? What if she did not like me?

She smiled at me, then walked in the other direction.

I pounded away at the berries until there was another bowlful to empty. The sun swam almost directly over camp now. Dogs and babies played together, common as fleas in the warm dust. Still I watched, but no one came.

One time a group of four younger girls strolled by, giggling and talking. Were they ever lucky to be free and lazy today.

I noticed them looking sideways at the red-spotted tipi. They walked back and forth in front of it, but I doubted if they were admiring the design. I knew who they wanted to see.

I pounded my berries harder and did not watch them. It was hard not to see what they were doing, though. They stood laughing together, ignoring me the whole time, before they headed off.

One girl, the skinny one, dragged behind her friends to moon at the spotted tipi some more. At last, her eyes caught mine, and I gave her a stare. As I was sitting by my father's tipi I could watch whatever I wanted, but she had to leave or people would notice her lingering.

My legs were squashed so dead by now that I could ignore their aching. They were almost not there. Fortunately, my berries were nearly all pounded. The last bag began to collapse from the top as I emptied it. Finally it fell over flat. Only one more bowlful.

I was almost finished, yet neither Favorite-Child nor my dear friend had come. Had they all forgotten me? Soon my almost-mother would call me to work inside the tipi, and from there I would not be able to see anybody. It seemed that not only the day, but summer itself was slipping away from me.

Soon my tribe would split into bands for our autumn hunting, or even into separate families, to spread over the land and make the best use of what little food we could scrounge in the cold of winter. For six or seven long moons I would not see Eagle-Sun. The very thought made me stare blurry-eyed into my berries. The only things that happened, it seemed, were things I could not touch or change.

What was that sound? It echoed somewhere inside me. Footsteps in the dust coming my way.

I hung my head in modest silence. This way I could still see the earth ahead and any moccasins that approached. Surely I knew those long slim feet?

They walked by me without pausing. All my insides crumpled, and deep within I could feel fire shooting up as it would within the dry trunk of a dead tree. I would die here, waiting. No one would ever come.

"Sweetgrass?"

Eagle-Sun's deep voice was soft, a powerful whisper. He stopped only a few steps away. I stared into the dust of his footprints, as was proper. But the quickening rise and fall of my shoulders must have shown him I was listening.

"I wondered . . . some of us thought we would meet to play toss ball. By the river, when the sun is almost ready to come down. I wondered if . . . if you would be there as well?"

In the pause that followed, I found I could not speak.

He added with half a laugh, "What I meant to say is, you always were good at toss ball."

Aiii. He was nervous just like me! Eagle-Sun, the young warrior, was not so very different from Eagle-Sun, my childhood playmate.

I looked up at him, and met his dark, deep eyes with their thick, short fringe of black eyelashes. When we look at each other, it is always just like this. We do not need to speak to show what we are feeling.

Shyly I lowered my head. What other trails might Eagle-Sun be able to follow in my eyes?

As softly as I could, I whispered, "I will be there, Eagle-Sun."

That was enough. His footsteps moved away quietly. They had a lift to them, I imagined, as if they longed to move to some old-time lover's flutesong outside a hushed tipi. To that same song my spirit yearned as well.

I hummed as I ground the last of the red berries. The berrymasher swirled around inside its mortar proudly, describing the shape of the sun. Almost done! The afternoon of the day shone bright all around me.

I could not help myself, but I felt so complete I laughed right out loud.

The laugh echoed behind me. I froze.

Had some disapproving old one been watching us? Would the news get to my father?

I slid a sneaking glance behind me. It *was* Father!

He laughed again, and his amusement was so big it shook his willow backrest against the wall of our tipi. Little-Brother was yawning sleepy-eyed in Father's lap. Had they been there all along? Had Eagle-Sun seen Father there . . . and talked to me anyway?

"So, daughter, you have a sweetheart!"

A blush prickled up over my shoulders to my down-turned cheeks. Eagle-Sun and I had not done anything against the old ways. I would not be ashamed.

Little-Brother broke the tension in the air. "Can Sweetgrass come too, Father?" A dimpled hand patted my father's shirtfront.

"Where are you going?" I knew the answer already, but asked anyway.

"To watch them build the Sun Dance lodge. All Blackfoot children should see the proper way to do it," said my father as he set Little-Brother down and brushed the dirt from the little boy's finely beaded ceremonial leggings, "but if you feel you are old enough to be married, you had better stay and become used to hard work."

A good Blackfoot girl never says disobedient things to her parents, but, oh, she thinks them! Father's eyes looked at me sharply. Eagle-Sun. I must not say it.

I lowered my eyes and stood silent, and Father limped away. Little-Brother ran after him, calling. He caught up to his father, then turned to raise a small hand to me. Good-bye.

I raised my blistered hand in return. Good-bye, Little-Brother.

Putting my work tools away was a quick job, but it was dark in the tipi and I had to do it all by feel. I squashed the bags together, then stacked others on top of them as high as they would go. I could tell even in the dark when a bag was going to fall over; it would push softly back against my hesitating fingers.

There. Done. Now only the mortar and berrymasher remained to be moved, and they were much heavier.

I bent and lifted the gray stone bowl, pulling it onto my knee. A little black slug slithered away from underneath. I put both my arms under and lifted it to where I could smell the damp earth on its bottom. I staggered through the door and thumped it down inside.

These tools could have their rest; I would have to

work till evening. But tonight there would be games and dances. Tonight, and for the next few nights!

Father was wrong. I *did* work hard already. He did not understand that I would be working with the power of a married woman in me. There would be more joy in my bitterness, there *must* be, living with Eagle-Sun. Father was just oozing the unhappiness of his own bad leg.

That was what Favorite-Child said, too, when she arrived.

"What does it matter if your father saw you talking with a young man?" My cousin was wearing her mother's important look of someone giving serious advice.

"Will you help me put the berrymasher away?" I asked. "I am really tired."

"Yes. Remember, Eagle-Sun is a fine young warrior."

I lifted the arm-long wooden handle that the berrymasher's stone head was tied to, and backed through the tipi hole.

"I bet your father thinks Eagle-Sun is a fine young man. So why not flirt with him? Your father will marry you to Eagle-Sun," said Favorite-Child, casually pushing her end of the pestle into the tipi, "or to someone else."

The heavy stone head fell with a thump, almost cracking my big toe.

"Oh, did you nearly get hurt? You have a very heavy masher. Your mother should get a lighter one." She held the flap for me to climb out. "My mother is always saying how lucky you are. She says her brother Shabby-Bull will be careful to get his daughter a fine husband."

"A good husband like Pretty-Girl's father chose for her?"

"Aiii, Sweetgrass! You know that's different. Pretty-Girl's father is a good-for-nothing *kimataps.*"

At that, I just about gagged. I do not like you, Favorite-Child, I thought. I like Pretty-Girl. I like her even though she has no powerful family to go crying to.

I held my tongue. Evening would come soon enough. Tonight we would play toss ball and all the voices would sing out in excitement. My anger seeped slowly away.

Favorite-Child and I gossiped while the sun made its way down through the cloud-patched sky. One thing she told me was very good: she had heard news about Pretty-Girl. One of her own older sisters had gone gathering wild mint with Pretty-Girl and some others in the morning. Pretty-Girl had proudly announced that Five-Killer would recount his mighty war deeds tomorrow evening after the ceremonies. And so, my cousin added, would her own famous father.

At the back of the lodge, where the unmarried women sit in the shadows by the great lodge door, we would barely be able to hear the stories. But we all knew them by heart. The exciting part was the acting-out. When the men told their stories, they also showed how things happened.

Favorite-Child and I laughed when we remembered the best tale, the time Crazy-Bear had Chief Shoots-Back of the Crow tribe as a guest. For some odd reason we were not fighting the Crows then. Crazy-Bear acted out a famous fight he had had with his Crow guest.

They told it to us from the beginning. We all had heard what happened, but it was a fine thing to see.

The two of them portrayed the Blood attack on the

enemy camp. They acted out Chief Shoots-Back awakening; our warrior's brave resistance; Crazy-Bear finally galloping rifleless out to hide in the hills with all his friends dead behind him. Crazy-Bear gave us a good fierce recital. You could see he was getting deep into the spirit of the day!

Then Shoots-Back showed how he trailed the galloping horse out of camp, how he crept through the sage after the escaping Blood warrior. I dug my fingernails into my hands, watching them. When Crazy-Bear jumped from his canyon hiding place onto Shoots-Back, the whole Sun Dance crowd gasped—a big sound like the wind before thunder. The enemies wrestled back and forth.

First our warrior was on top, then the other. Crazy-Bear made a pretend-move with his knife. Shoots-Back forced down his wrist. The strangled hand grew purple. Our valiant warrior gave all his strength to the battle.

Then, as so many years before, the Crow chief's grip started trembling. Shoots-Back lowered his head. He bit Crazy-Bear's arm to distract him. Then, as so many years before, Crazy-Bear brought down his knife and knife-arm hard upon his enemy's head.

Only this time he brought it down harder. Shoots-Back's skull cracked. This time he was dead.

The Crows never made peace with us again for a long time!

The Sun Dance is always exciting. More than anything else, Favorite-Child and I wanted to be Sun Dance Women someday.

A Sun Dance Woman is a great woman who has asked a big thing from the sun, and Sun has made it true. Then she makes the Dance go right next year. But it is very hard. If anything goes wrong, we know the Sun Dance Woman is weak and bad, and she has brought bad luck on us all.

Nothing went wrong the summer my aunt Robe-Woman was Sun Dance sponsor. Everything went as it was supposed to. I saw my aunt fasting and praying in her tipi for the four days. She made the big lodgepole slide into its place straight and true. When people talk about old happenings, they mark when it was by saying—aiii, yes that was when Robe-Woman was sponsor. A beautiful ceremony, they say. Everyone remembers.

My aunt Robe-Woman has honor forever. She has proved to all the people her virtue and her power with the Sun. I wanted to be chosen Sun Dance Woman someday, too. Or at least I wanted to help at the Sun Dance, or give a fine gift to the Sun to thank Him for giving me power.

Many women gave smaller gifts. If the Sun brought a woman's husband home safe from a war-party, she might give a fine dress that she vowed to Him.

Grandmother once vowed a finger-joint from her next baby if the Sun made the baby live and grow. Four of her babies before that died. But He made this baby live. When he was still a small child, Grandmother gave the gift promised. That is why my father has a short left-middle finger.

My cousin expected to give the Sun many gifts when she was married, just like her mother did. But Favorite-Child preferred not to talk about other women and the ceremony, but about the gifts the young warriors offered up.

"This year Four-Bulls—you do not know him, Sweetgrass, he is a warrior from a southern band—vowed to swing on a loop tied from the lodgepole through his chest muscles till they rip off. Without fainting! Do you think he can do it?"

I did not even know Four-Bulls, but he seemed a real boaster to say he could do it without fainting.

"Of course other young men have given gifts that good. Did you see Eagle-Sun's Sun Dance gift three summers ago?" She paused for a moment but rattled on, ignoring my silence.

"They say the Sun has favored him ever since. What do *you* think, Sweetgrass? They say Eagle-Sun owns almost enough horses to ask for a wife."

So this was the news my cousin had for me.

I looked up to see her staring hard at my face. She had her eyes open big as if she was asking me a question. No, I did *not* want to talk about this. I did not want to gather my feelings and set them out for display. Especially for her. My cousin looked away and flicked at the end of one long and shiny braid with a broken fingernail.

"I thought you wanted to hear what they say."

My cousin curled her braid around her finger. Into her strong black hair she had tied meadow flowers and bright cloth pieces from the trader. She always had everything. I said nothing to her.

Finally she spoke again, in a high sharp voice this time. "I'm glad not to be marrying such a very young warrior."

I said nothing.

"My promised husband never goes on the raiding trail. He doesn't have to because his father, a chief, has maybe a thousand horses already. No bad luck can make me a young widow!"

Again I said nothing.

"I am going to be a Sun Dance Woman. I will own enough horses and I will have enough wives under me. I will be important enough to lift that holy burden. Sweetgrass, you will see me in the elkskin Sun Dance robe, giving blessings to all the people. You will see."

At that point Almost-Mother came over and scolded me for not helping when she was so busy. She gave me a buffalo calf's hide to make ready for scraping. Favorite-Child wandered off. I was glad to work. Now I did not have to listen.

Toss ball that evening was just as I remembered it from my earlier Sun Dances. We made a circle, boys and girls, and threw the hard hair-stuffed ball from person to person. It took a real struggle to keep that ball off the ground. Otter tried hardest. This was the first year we had let him play. Once he threw himself under the ball and it smashed his nose. The blood looked funny, trickling down around his surprised mouth and onto his chin, so we all laughed to buck him up. Otter kept playing, but he was more careful after that. A fine warrior, my brother.

As ever, Favorite-Child was at the middle of the flirting. That thin girl who was always the best player was there. She looked at Eagle-Sun often. But I was proud to notice that Eagle-Sun usually passed the ball to me whenever he got it.

I watched him. He watched me. It was fun, the old toss ball game. Mostly it is a time for girls and boys to laugh and flirt together. Why did Pretty-Girl have to marry? I missed her at my elbow.

But this time, the night after the game was different. Before, I had always walked back to the camp, laughing and chattering with my girlfriends. I had already decided who I was going to walk with—Favorite-Child and her friends, not that skinny girl. However, this year, Eagle-Sun asked me to stay, so I didn't join the other girls when they gathered to go home.

There were other young men and women staying by the river. All of them were promised couples. I knew some of them: Dog-Leg and his wife-to-be were among the few. In the old times, by what the storytellers said, there would have been many. Few marrying nowadays came from ages so close to each other. Catching my look by chance, Dog-Leg smiled at me and Eagle-Sun.

My throat, my face did *not* burn. Let everyone see us together! I was *not* ashamed.

Eagle-Sun and I walked along together in silence while the night grew stranger and stranger. The grass under our moccasins glowed gold and green in the setting sun while the sky over our heads flooded slowly to purple. It felt like a spirit-world, but I did not say so.

Eagle-Sun found us a dry log by the river, and he sat down on it. Should I sit, too? It was safe. Other people were near us. Still, in the dusky light he looked like somebody else entirely, not my long-known sweetheart. And he sat very close to me. How could I talk to him?

"Eagle-Sun?" I whispered. This was not unfolding as it did in my dreams.

The dark figure beside me rubbed his buckskin leggings softly, sending off a sound like dry leaves turning in the wind.

"Sweetgrass." Eagle-Sun's voice came from the dark stranger's face. "You're wearing the incense we burn in the winter. I like its perfume."

"You like it?" I did not know what else to say.

"Do you remember how I tied some into a fly whisk for your pony once? You were just a skinny little girl. I thought of you last winter when we burned some dry sweetgrass."

"I thought about you, too. Even when I did not see any eagles. That was a bad winter."

Beside us the river mumbled. Its wind smelled of something I did not recognize. Everywhere was dark tonight.

"A bad winter," nodded Eagle-Sun. "I tracked a moose through the snow for three days. It was so cold that the sky, the trees, everything, shone like bitter ice. I thought I would go blind, Sweetgrass, it hurt my eyes so much."

"Aiii. I hear you."

"Finally I broke in on a Piegan camp. When I stepped through their tipi flap, they were all looking at me. But their eyes were frozen open. I wanted to die, too. My shadow longed to join the others in the Sand Hills."

"No, Eagle-Sun!" I touched his hands gently to find

no warmth in them. "Do not long for the deadland. It is not right to greet death, except in battle."

"I know."

"Every year spring comes again. . . ."

"Hear me, Sweetgrass. If you were my woman . . ."

"Yes?"

We hunched together against the wet river wind which was gusting over the dark plains that night.

Someday soon we would be together. Who knew what would come, but I would be ready. My whole body felt alive when I was near Eagle-Sun. With him I could do anything, touch the spirits and make them speak to me, keep him safe with my power.

Someday it would happen. Eagle-Sun told me that my parents had spoken well to the asker he had sent. They had almost said yes. But when would my parents agree I was old enough to marry? When the leaves fell? When they furled open again to a new spring? We could only wait.

Or must we? Slowly an idea budded, stirring tight-wrapped inside of me.

# 7

# A KETTLE OF STEW

ON THE LAST AFTERNOON OF THE SUN DANCE I hovered over our stew kettle. It smelled good. The aromas of rabbit, prairie chicken and buffalo meat joined with the sharper smells of wild turnip and wild onion, dried berries, mushrooms and a handful of spicy leaves for good flavoring. Father, surely, would have to like it.

He would not refuse anything to his dutiful daughter, would he?

Tomorrow Eagle-Sun was going north. He had sent me word. He and his friends were taking dried meat and fox and wolf skins to Fort Edmonton, the English trading post on the North Saskatchewan River.

Such a long journey! Our Sun Dance camp was closer to the American traders on the Marias River than to the English, but the English gave the biggest price for small skins, and they needed winter meat more, too. The Americans gave the most for buffalo robes. My father often traveled south to them in the winter.

Eagle-Sun was off north. Everyone needed guns and bullets and metal arrowheads for the fall buffalo hunts, so when he came back with the trade goods he would be able to exchange them for many horses. Fiercely I promised myself that is how things would be. Father could not refuse a loving daughter, or a suitor with many fine horses, now could he?

My almost-mother came and sniffed at my stew kettle. "Umm. Good eating, Sweetgrass."

I thought she looked at me strangely. Maybe she was surprised to see me make such good food. I didn't usually get up earlier than she did and gather flavoring leaves from the wet meadow. And I didn't usually fill the whole kettle, either. The prairie chicken had come to my snares as I asked it to. So had the rabbits. Today everything was going my way.

Almost-Mother had even let me take dried turnips and berries from our storage bags without protest. All afternoon she worked at beading a lucky butterfly-of-dreams figure on my new ceremonial dress. Yes, today was looking fine.

Except in one regard. Robe-Woman. She came to talk with my almost-mother, and they both looked at me and shook their heads. May her hair-grease stink! I would never say that out loud, though. I am a good Blackfoot woman and follow the proper ways of duty.

And no one should be suspicious of me.

So I stirred my kettle, my face turned modestly down. Soon the old women spoke of other things. They chatted, I stirred, and the afternoon rode peacefully away from us. At long last, Robe-Woman had unpacked her load of gossip. She heaved her great carcass up, panting, and carefully squeezed out our tipi flap.

That left Almost-Mother and me alone together, alone except for the littlest baby, and babies do not count. Grandmother had gone out earlier with Little-Brother to visit old friends and say her words of parting. One of the bands was leaving tomorrow for the foothills, and we likely would not see them at the fall hunts.

The Sun Dance camp was almost ended. So quickly. And I had hoped for so much from this Sun Dance. Many girls had married, but not me. I still lived in my almost-mother's tipi. At least now I knew Eagle-Sun wished to have me.

I held out a hope that his band would camp with mine until winter. Many good things could happen. If only my sweetheart could trade for our horses before two or three moons had passed . . .

Almost-Mother stopped sewing to rethread her needle. "Don't you think Wears-Trade-Dress-Woman sponsored a fine ceremony, Sweetgrass? Such a virtuous woman she is, even though her sister is always running away with new husbands. The things that childless women may do!"

She paused to push the needle carefully through the thin leather of my new dress. "Robe-Woman says that sister left her last husband only because he horsewhipped her a little too often."

"What does Robe-Woman say about Wears-Trade-Dress-Woman?"

"I have never said Wears-Trade-Dress-Woman herself was not virtuous! You know I have not. No, she is a very fine woman."

"Of course. She is the Sun Dance Woman."

"You must try to be like her. I hope someday to see you assisting the sponsor of a fine ceremony."

Did she hope to see me *sponsoring* a fine ceremony? I did not ask. Almost-Mother talked about many things that afternoon, sounding like the rattles at a dance, beating faster and faster, never stopping.

All the midsummer visiting had made her talkative. Her eyes sparkled as she looked at my new dress. "I remember when I was a girl I had a fine dress like this, with a lucky butterfly on the back. It brought good dreams. What color do you want for the wings of your butterfly?"

"Whatever color brings the most luck." A daring and improper question burned on my lips. My almost-mother was in one of her kind moods, so she might answer.

Tell me, I willed with all my strength.

"How long did it take your butterfly to bring you the luck of a husband?" I asked, and held my breath.

Almost-Mother dropped the red bead she was sewing. It rolled away on the ground cover. She sighed. I waited, saying nothing.

I watched her poke at the tiny hole in the bead with the tip of her needle. It just rolled away from her, but she kept poking at it. I waited through all this. At last Almost-Mother picked the bead up in her fingers and dropped it down the needle's shiny length. It fell down the thread and dangled, a little red splash at the bottom against the soft beige suede. She started sewing again.

I sighed to show I was still waiting, which was rude. But rude or not, I somehow had to force her to answer.

"Even luck needs patience, Sweetgrass."

"If I am patient and the butterfly brings me dreams of a husband, then will they come true? When will they come true?"

"Aiii! What is wrong with you, girl? Dreams are always true. But you know dreams are spirit things. If you cannot catch the winds of knowing in your own heart, then do not ask me." Almost-Mother drew in her breath, shook her head, and continued, "The mighty *na-tose* Eagle-Legs long ago said . . ."

There was a rustling at the tipi flap and Otter stepped into view. I glared at him but he did not take the hint. He just glared back. Almost-Mother was rescued.

Instead of leaving as I wanted him to do, Otter approached the kettle in that weaselly way of his and wrinkled his nose.

"What is that bad smell, Mother?" he asked. "Someone drop a piece of leather in the fire? Someone forgot to change the baby?"

He started pulling pieces out of the kettle with his fingers, and sniffing at them like a dog at maggoty meat. Almost-Mother tried to stop him.

"What did you put in here, Sweetgrass? Fresh buffalo chips? You can trust me, I will not tell Father. Bear fat?"

"Otter, stop!" I cried.

"Mother, I bet I have found it. Do you know what Sweetgrass put in the kettle?" He held up a long dripping piece of white turnip. "Fish!"

Oh, was I angry! I thought my stomach would come up through my mouth. How dare he! How dare he accuse me of serving *that*! No Blackfoot eats fish. It is a forbidden food. Just thinking about it made me ill. My lovely tasty stew!

"You, you, you, Otter," I blurted out, "you are so much of an otter you would even eat fish."

He blinked at me.

"You even think stew is fish!" I hissed. "Oh, go down to your river and dive in. I hope you drown!"

But the shock on Otter's face did not last long.

"Daughter, my daughter," said a deep, reproachful voice behind me.

My back stiffened. To be caught like this . . .

Father bent through the tipi flap.

"You behave like naughty quarreling cubs. I should threaten you with the Bear maybe coming. Do you remember the Bear, my woman?" He was laughing and wobbly on his feet.

"Yes, I remember," said Almost-Mother. She seemed to have a hard time forcing her words out.

Then a sharp, foreign smell reached my nose. Some Piegan warrior must have brought skins full of trader's whiskey. Father might act strangely. All of us had to be careful.

We backed away from the kettle.

"That stew has a fine smell," said Father with a grand gesture. "Son, you must be polite to your sister or she will not let you eat from the good kettle. Ha! There may be no pieces left big enough to pick up when I have finished."

He laughed again. If only it were safe to laugh with him!

Otter sulked while Father pulled out hunk after hunk

of meat and vegetable, sucking his fingers after each to show his liking. It could have been that my almost-brother had not eaten yet today. Almost-Mother and I had stolen cold chunks from the kettle bottom before refilling it. That, with tasting each thing as it went into the water or as it bubbled up cooking, made my stomach feel solid. I was not hungry. Leftover broth eaten with a horn spoon would be good enough for me.

At last my father finished eating and stretched out. Otter slid over to poke quietly in the pot. There *was* something. I waited to see what he would leave for us, the women.

Father said at long last, "That was good food. Lucky is the man with such a cook for a wife." Slowly he filled his pipe with trade tobacco.

Here was my chance.

"Father, when would such a man have such a wife? While the leaves still have some green in them?"

My father hauled his legs in under him to balance himself for rising. His pipe tipped and spilled its hot ash on his leggings. I saw Otter watching from his place at the kettle. We all held our breath and waited. Tell me, oh, tell me. I pulled at Father's spirit with mine. Tell me.

"You know I will choose for you carefully," he growled. "Otter, get me more tobacco! This pipe has a hole in the bottom."

"Father—"

"Be silent, Sweetgrass."

Winter ice touched my heart at his words. Father might yet choose a wealthy man for my husband.

There was no meat left in the stew pot.

That night I sat at the very back of the great Sun Dance lodge, listening to the stories. Five-Killer, the great warrior, was talking about his brave deeds. He had just finished telling of his trip down the Missouri River on the American white man's steamboat.

"When I got off the steamboat I saw many things. I visited our brother-tribe the Mandans. Hear me! I will tell you what I saw. The Mandans are the people who live in round-topped tipis. They are the people who scratch in the earth. Not like us; they have little meat from the buffalo, little *real* food to eat. They scratch in the earth and grow other food, food like the wild plants our women dig from the prairie."

That sounded interesting. Maybe someday Eagle-Sun would take me there. Men and women sometimes travel together on far journeys.

"This earth-food they fed to me," said Five-Killer. "Oh, brothers, I was a sad man, away from my people!

"But the Mandans have many trade goods. Their great chief felt honored that I visited him. This Mandan chief felt honored, so he gave me many trade goods. He gave me six fine red blankets. He gave me this metal finger ring. He gave me . . ."

I yawned. We had heard this all before. Five-Killer always tells this tale to the lodge each summer, and he lists the gifts exactly the same way. Still, most of the people around me looked like they were listening.

I saw Eagle-Sun's mother and father, but I couldn't see Eagle-Sun. Probably he was sorting his furs for tomorrow's journey.

Eagle-Sun. My thoughts slid toward him. My husband-to-be, hurry back from the north. Buy many strings of fine horses. Hurry, hurry, winter is coming.

I imagined my sweetheart leading fine horses to Father's tipi. I pictured Father coming out, smiling and greeting him. I tied the spirit-pictures together firmly. I could see it all, exactly as it would be. Hear me, Sun. Hear my desire. See it. Let this be.

One moment the picture was clear as a reflection in water; the next, it turned to shattered ice. Someone had touched me.

I snapped back to the dim time and place where my body still lived. Where was I? In the darkness, with fuzzy rows of people before me. Ah, still the Sun Dance lodge.

"Are you all right, Sweetgrass?" asked my cousin Favorite-Child. She smiled at me with glowing eyes while I forced myself to wake and look at her.

"What do you want?"

"Did I wake you? Eagle-Sun told my brother Dog-Leg I was to bring you a message. A scout from your band found buffalo today. Our people are going west to meet them tomorrow, or maybe the day after that. The Sun Dance is over and the time for gathering winter meat has come."

Favorite-Child was so annoying. She never told me anything in a straight line.

"The time for gathering winter meat has come. That is something I know. What is your message?"

"Eagle-Sun says his mother wants to pick berries first, in the valleys, before they hunt for buffalo. But his father has promised to follow our bands later. So Eagle-Sun says he will see you again before the moon has grown and faded."

Favorite-Child laughed. I stared at her.

"Oh, Sweetgrass! Do you think your father will let you marry before the bands split for winter?"

# 8

# THE BUFFALO

THERE WAS NOTHING TO DO BUT WAIT. I PICKED AND throw the remaining days of summer behind me, one by one like prairie chicken feathers. My band hunted with my uncle's band. I kept watch for Eagle-Sun. For the next whole moon our scouts found many buffalo.

They covered the prairie. My brother said they were thick as fleas on a dog's back. "Yes!" laughed my almost-mother. She was so happy because the buffalo were fast filling our food bags. Much is needed against the winter, a wife knows. Winter is a hungry time.

When the first snow falls, the buffalo seem to vanish. The plains become empty. Game then is scarce, even inside the quiet, tangled cold of our forests. High wind and snow slow down the hunters more than you would think. Sometimes they die of cold or by the treachery of the ice.

That is why women pack winter pemmican bags. The men seem to worry less about starving to death.

The storing of food kept me busy while I waited. Eagle-Sun's people would join us soon now, or so we were told. I waited one moon and then another. Eagle-Sun should be riding back from the north now with our arrowheads and guns. I built fire racks, smoked buffalo meat and sewed our furry winter moccasins. My strength came from knowing he would soon come. One thing alone troubled me. My almost-mother kept running her hands over the dirty edges of our tipi cover.

Old and worn, it should be replaced before too long. But the making of a new one took two women working hard through half a winter. Too much work for Almost-Mother to do alone. She might decide not to let me marry before winter. What could I do to turn her mind from the tipi cover?

I cut knobby burls from ash-tree trunks for her. They are good for winter carving. If you carve them in the right way, the bowls will have the woodgrain swirling around inside. Robe-Woman owned several. Perhaps Almost-Mother might like some?

She accepted my offer with a nod only. "I will be busy enough this winter, my daughter." It did not look good for me.

At last an autumn sharpness came into the air. It hurt to breathe, a little. Hard breathing means winter coming on.

"Frost prickles you, Sweetgrass?" teased my aunt Robe-Woman.

She knew. Prickly is how frost feels, like plant burrs against my insides, like my fear of the nearness of winter.

My aunt laughed. "You should pay Frost no attention, Sweetgrass. Soon enough he will be sending arrows!"

I waited.

Then one afternoon, as I worked alone in an empty camp, I was surprised by the sound of someone shouting my name. I looked up from the dried strips of meat I was pounding. Everyone except maybe one or two old ones were away at the hunt site. The shouts echoed through the camp silence around me.

"Sweetgrass," a child shouted.

She was running in the grassy distance. I squinted to see her. She had a small face, a big smile, and a scar across her forehead.

Her hair was hacked short for mourning some dead person. It was not a new cut; no, it had grown out somewhat. Loud-Daughter, the youngest of Favorite-Child's almost-sisters! Yes, I recognized her. She was special among the horde of small faces, a pet of Favorite-Child's, the one who ran her errands. Loud-Daughter had indeed earned her name. Even the last deaf dog in camp must have heard her calling.

"Sweetgrass, Sweetgrass, hear me. My sister gave me a message to bring you," Loud-Daughter gasped out as she ran, smiling with pride in her errand.

She stumbled trying to stop. I grabbed one small ankle so she wouldn't fall over.

Holding her hands before her, she solemnly repeated the message: "Favorite-Child says she greets you. She asks why are you working in camp? Everyone else is loading buffalo meat on horse travois. None by dog."

I pounded pemmican as I listened. Bang, bang, bang. Favorite-Child was as overbearing by messenger as she was in person. Why did she want me out at the hunt?

"Favorite-Child says there is much meat to pack because her men have killed almost all the buffalo by the Plenty Hills. You should be there to help. There are so few buffalo left that the scouts say they will go find more.

"Favorite Child says to tell you that the scouts also found people."

"Who did they find?"

"I have to tell you the way my sister told me to."

"Just tell me your message."

"Hear me, cousin. My sister says . . . she says . . . you will be *interested* in these special people. I was supposed to tell you that, and all the other things first, and then tell you that the people our scouts met are none other than Eagle-Sun's family! They are riding to our hunt site, Favorite-Child says." Loud-Daughter at long last drew a deep breath. I could not help notice her eyeing my handiwork.

"May I have a piece of that dried meat for telling you?"

I flipped her a piece. "You tell a brave and important story. But it would be better told more quickly."

She waited while I put my tools away. Then we turned toward the hunt site. Loud-Daughter sucked on her meat strip as we walked along. She made a strange noise with it. Probably the grasshoppers stared at us.

The prairie rustled its long grassy coat as we pushed through it. We made our own trail. When I was a child I used to count the many kinds of grass. Almost every stalk was different. Some were tan and others soft green. There were sharp green, yellow, dead brown and many more. Some of them whipped me around the ankles, while taller ones tickled the backs of my knees. Some even reached up to slap at my elbows. I liked the ones with round beads at their tops for looks, but for chewing, the ones with the sharp tight seedcones, or the ones with long floppy brushes, if you were careful. That afternoon Loud-Daughter counted nine kinds of grass. I counted twelve.

Then Favorite-Child's pet wanted to count sounds (grasshopper, gray-brown toad, hawk dives), or smells (campfires, grassfires, stale water), or animal burrows—too many! With much relief I sighted the vultures.

They were riding wind currents over a hill, near the setting sun. Vultures are always black against bright sun like that. They would be dreaming eating dreams directly above our kill.

They knew us. We would leave meaty bones for their feasting. Blackfoot and vultures share the buffalo, just like buffalo and rabbits share the grasses.

Loud-Daughter and I climbed the hill toward them. The earth was bloody wet with killing. Huge brown bodies stained the green grasses. Our bellies would be full tonight! The chattering child and I walked down toward the people and they heard us coming.

Everyone worked busily. I saw Favorite-Child first, bending over some leg bones with a knife in her hand. She was cutting off meat hunks for drying. Loud-Daughter ran down to her almost-sister. I raised my hand to greet her and walked on, frowning to the west. Favorite-Child had been a good friend to me this time but . . . Lucky for me she was busy with another friend of hers working beside her. Aiii, it was the thin girl who always looked at Eagle-Sun with big eyes. She smiled at me and I smiled back. Favorite-Child beckoned with a smile. I signed that I must go to where Almost-Mother worked, and kept on going.

Almost-Mother would need me. I could see her small figure bending over something, another hill over in the direction of the sun. She was loading up travois.

This particular one was hitched to a horse almost as skinny-legged and swollen-bellied as the old woman holding its bridle. As I came nearer I could see that the poor animal had a stinking skin ulcer and a crowd of eager flies.

She really should do something about that horse.

As the old woman's eyes met mine, I made my greeting respectfully. Then I touched Almost-Mother gently on the elbow.

"Where are the new people?" I asked. "Did another band not come to join our hunt?"

"Oh, there you are, Sweetgrass. I am happy you are here. Your father and Otter have been killing so many buffalo! Otter shot a great fat cow just now. One, two, three, four legs, a hide, and the back hump. Yes, that is right." She paused to check the loaded travois, then waved the old widow to lead the horse away.

"Now, what was I just saying? Oh, Otter shot a great cow. So big, his first full-sized buffalo! So young—to have his dream *come true.* Your father was right to let him ride in the hunt this year."

"Did someone say it was wrong?"

"That fat Robe-Woman. Otter's riding is as good as any young man's. Why should he only shoot at calves on the herd-edge? Your father was right. Wait till I show you Otter's cow you are going to butcher."

"All alone, Almost-Mother?"

"Alone. I am busy."

"Could you not come with me?"

"If my son can kill a buffalo, then my almost-grown daughter can butcher it."

She brought me the tools, mostly trader's metal, not stone like the old ones. Nice.

"I have to finish this bull here. Our poor old relative came over the hill with her travois before I was finished my first work. Your father will be pleased I gave that cow to her. She left the tongue and the soft pieces for him, too, just as is right." Almost-Mother sharpened the knife for me, spitting on the flat rock from time to time.

"You were saying something, Sweetgrass? About another family arriving. Maybe I should not ask how you heard that?"

My shoulders turned red. Almost-Mother grinned, and poked me gently with the butt of the knife.

"It is so. Eagle-Sun's family moves this way."

Quickly and neatly, my almost-mother wrapped the buffalo's heart, sweetbread, brains and liver in a bit of hide. She thrust them at me to load on the travois.

"Eagle-Sun, of course, is not yet back from Fort Edmonton."

I kicked through the flowers in disgust. There were rivers of them running over the hills between Otter's great buffalo and the main hunt. Almost-Mother had no feelings for me. I had waited so patiently and not said a word. But Eagle-Sun would come soon now. I knew it. Yellow asters and wild blue lupines nodded in the breeze.

It was, after all, a sun-dipped day, with the late afternoon light filling everything with a golden glow. Happiness could not help but open inside me.

Even Otter's tough old cow could not discourage me. She had fallen hard on her side in the grass, squashing a clump of bushes. One late wild rose peeked out from under her. What a big job to be given.

Nobody had started the heavy butchering work. The men must be so busy they had not reached this far. I would have to cut through the main joints myself.

I saw Otter looking down at me from the top of the next hill. I could hear faint yells, and sometimes a gun cracking over there, behind him. I noticed Otter had exchanged his slow-shooting flintlock for a bow and arrow like most of the other men. He ought to be using them, not watching me. Probably he wanted to admire his buffalo.

Putting the tools down on the grass, I walked around her for a better look. Where to start cutting? The air was rank with blood and animal fear. Otter was still watching from his hill. Of course he would not come down and help. Was one buffalo not enough kill for him? I wished he would go back to the hunt and leave me alone.

His cow lay on her right side with her head to me. She was at least twenty or twenty-five times my weight. Her head was as long as my arm.

Her great black eyes stared back from under rough curls. Aiii, I thought, maybe the Mandans are right, scratching food out of the dirt. But no, a Blackfoot woman knows we have to eat some buffalo or other. The hunters make promises to the spirits. This was our way, the way we had always done it.

Maybe an ax blow against that brown shoulder?

One quick stroke should part both skin and muscle, showing me where to split the shoulder joint through soft cartilage past the bone. I had never butchered anything that size before.

I chose my target carefully. There, where a faint ridge showed the skeleton's weakness under the fur.

Swinging the ax high above my head, I held it for a moment, balancing, aiming. Then I drove it down with all my might. The ax bit deep, cleaving skin and blood and bone.

The buffalo rose up, snorting furiously, my ax still sticking in her! Impossible!

Her eyes were wide with pain and anger. I leapt back. When she shook, the earth trembled underfoot. A dark mountain of fur rippled in front of me and shut out the sun. Where could I go?

We were caught together in a cup of the hills.

Back away. Back away slowly. Slowly, slowly, windward of her.

Father had once said that buffalo can see only a little distance.

Her sides heaved as she gathered breath. Slowly, slowly I edged backward. Maybe she would not see me. Maybe she would not feel my movement.

But then the monstrous head swiveled, and her big, bloody eye fixed upon me. There was no mistake about it.

She charged.

The darkness loomed down on me, and I remember nothing more.

Coward! Sun vibrated inside my skull. Some great

power pressed down on my body. If I could only push my eyelids open, then I could shuffle off this pain.

Coward, but alive. The dim world ran with pain. If I hurt so much, I must be alive.

That buffalo must have charged over me. I was here, but my body was in a different place. My thoughts could not touch it.

There, down there, were my painful toes. And painful fingers. No way to move them. If my spirit was floating free, did that mean I was dead for sure?

I forced myself toward the buzzing voices.

I made my sticky eyes open.

A black sky was above me. Was this the spirit sky, the shadowland of dead things? I blinked to see better and found the black sky was curly fur, fur like on a buffalo. The creature was lying half on top of me. I was under my brother's buffalo.

The women and some hunters pulled her body off mine. She was completely dead at last, that cow buffalo of Otter's. The healer woman rubbed the spirit back into the rest of my body. No part of me was broken, she whispered in my ear.

Luck had protected me. Everyone said so, but they said much more about Otter.

Otter had been watching from the hilltop. He shouted when she rose and came galloping down the hill to my rescue. He sank an arrow into her heart when she turned on me. Father would hire an old man to ride through the camp telling the story. Otter saved his sister's life, they said. Sure . . . when it was all his fault for not killing the cow in the first place!

I was not grateful. Not at all grateful. How could I be?

Sewing and babywatching kept me busy while my body healed itself. It took me several days to slowly gather my spirit. Everyone was kind. Grandmother even sat at home, sometimes, and talked with me.

One morning we spread chokecherries together on hides laid around the tipi so they could dry in the gentle autumn sun. It was a fine day. The air was full of the scent of yellow leaves and sweet berries. The smoke from the meat-curing fires tickled the inside of my nose.

It was good. Grandmother rolled all the chokecherries over with her forked stick. That way they would dry evenly. Then she picked up her needle and resumed sewing.

"How do you like this new saddle I am making for my favorite grandson?"

I glanced at Otter's saddle and mumbled something polite.

"Why are you so angry with your almost-brother?"

"Everyone praises Otter for what he does. I could have killed that buffalo too if I had been up on a horse with a gun."

"Yes, I expect you could have killed it too. But why are you so angry?" Grandmother aimed her dark eyes at me.

"No one praises what I do, Grandmother."

"No one?"

"Not like they praise Otter. Father will never pay a herald to ride through camp and shout about me. 'Praises be to Sweetgrass, stewmaker and babywatch, slayer of the charging prairie chicken!'"

Grandmother smiled, but she did not laugh.

· 97 ·

A bitter coil turned in my chest. My brother moved things. He found the path, the way of things, and traveled it and had fine dreams and did great things. He had choices.

But Sun never heard me.

I looked at my old grandmother sinking stitch after stitch of thread into the leather. Long ago, Sun and people heard her. She once had great power.

"I could go to war like you, Grandmother."

"You could."

"But I do not want to be a warrior." It was hard to explain this. "Most warriors die young."

She-Fought-Them did not look at me. My toes squirmed inside my soft moccasins. She stretched her stick out in the fading sun and turned the chokecherries again.

The berries were partly dry now; some were red and some were black. It depended on how ripe they were. Grandmother turned them all. I was glad when she offered me a handful.

"Do all fall berries taste bitter, Granddaughter?" she asked with laughter in her eyes.

I imagine the face I made was funny. Chokecherries pucker your mouth and fill it full of cobwebs.

"It is the bitter berries that come to us just before the earth freezes." She looked deep into my eyes. "And bitter or not, we need them. What is the use of all Otter's buffalo, if you and I do not dry his meat? Yet no one will praise us. Some things must be done without sweet words."

She sewed calmly for a few stitches while I tightened

my mouth and thought my own thoughts. No matter what she said, the great She-Fought-Them had done much for praising. I would do so too.

"Hear me, Sweetgrass. Your wishes are not all without answers. Last night a young rider came into camp to join his family."

I looked up. Was the moon of my good fortune again growing full? For a moment I hoped.

"Yes," smiled my grandmother. "It was Eagle-Sun."

# 9

# FEVER ON THE WIND

Now autumn had fully come. A strong sun lit the twisting leaves above our heads, shone yellow-orange through their thinness as we walked by the river. Pretty-Girl and I went down to the river many times now. I had been so lonely for her.

Along the riverbank grew chokecherry bushes. Their bunches resisted only a moment, then surrendered red and black rivers into our hands.

Overhead the poplar leaves dragged briefly in the wind, then surrendered one by one. Their lost companions lay bruised under our feet, bleeding forth the clear, mind-sharpening smell of decay.

Eagle-Sun had ridden into camp the other night with fine goods from the traders. Early the next morning, he and his friends rode out again as I knew they would. This time they went south to the Piegans. There were among our southern brothers many gun buyers who would pay off in fine horses. The Piegan herds are famous everywhere.

Feeding horses is a problem in winter. Come cold

weather, a gun is a better companion. So in fall a young man with rifles could trade up to many wife-worthy horses. Please, let us need good horses, I asked inside. May my father like them.

A long way down the yellow fringes of the river—yet clear in my sight—were the rising southern hills. Maybe today, I hoped, we would see the black shapes of riders galloping down the faraway faces. Maybe today we would run giggling and panting back to the campsite. "Hear, Eagle-Sun rides!" All our camp would come running out to see.

For several afternoons we had watched the hills and waited. Once again, the sun's shadows grew long upon an empty day. Pretty-Girl took whole drooping clusters in her hands and evenly plucked the berries—raw red, in-between purple and ripe black. She was so patient. I swung myself around to shield her from the bitter wind that came whipping up from the river.

Pretty-Girl's body must not be chilled now.

"Ummm," my friend munched, her mouth purple from the berries.

"You like them? They are only fall berries."

"Summer walked past us slowly. That is what Five-Killer says." Pretty-Girl opened her mouth to another handful of sour berries.

"Slowly?" I laughed.

"You do not think so? Five-Killer says it is a sign winter will be hard this year."

I shaded my eyes with my hand and squinted toward the mountains like a near-sighted warrior. I spoke in the heavy tones of Five-Killer. "Your days of marriage have brought many things. Summer walked quick . . . but winter will see you walk slow and hard!"

Pretty-Girl blushed. She touched the new roundness of her body.

"You are a good friend to make me laugh. But I am worried. I really am. Scraping buffalo hides will be hard work with this baby."

"They will not make you work much. It is your first baby."

"But I am the newest wife. And two of the others are having babies this winter also. Maybe early spring. I am afraid, Sweetgrass." Her voice trailed off.

I put my arm around her shoulder. "And why is that?"

"Five-Killer will not care for me the way he does now," she said in a flat voice. "I am to become old and bear children."

Around us blew the sour wind of a late day in autumn. Pretty-Girl looked miserable. Weak fears stirred inside me.

"Aiii, Sweetgrass, I am so very tired."

No, Pretty-Girl, don't go on like this.

Five-Killer's other wives made my friend work from gray dawn to the dark blue sky of night. I knew that, but somehow it did not help to speak it out loud.

Another gust of wind whipped some of the yellow leaves from the tall river poplars. Their bending beauty was so painful and so sweet. The leaves fell from them like the silent footsteps of small animals, falling and falling away into the earth.

"Oh, Pretty-Girl, look at the leaves." She lifted her face under their gentle shower.

My friend must feel this too.

"Please do not worry about the winter," I begged. "Winter always walks back to spring, and I will help. Here, take some of my berries. Just sit and rest."

She stood twisting the end of one heavy braid, looking strangely at it with dull eyes. Coax her. Come, Pretty-Girl, smile with me!

"Next spring we can pick strawberries on the hills together. You will let me carry your baby sometimes, and I will tell you how happy I am to be married."

The corners of Pretty-Girl's mouth curled upward. I think she was just going to answer when a sound rang out in the evening air. It was the thudding echo of horses' hooves. Pretty-Girl was forgotten.

The excitement I longed for was coming. The river bushes made it hard to see, but I caught a glimpse. A band of men rode down the cleft in the southern hills.

Only three riders? The horses trotted chunkily through the brittle grass toward us. You could tell they were tired from a long journey. I grabbed a couple of berry bags and hurried to the edge of the berry patch for a clearer view.

"Pretty-Girl! Hurry! I'm going to need you as a chaperone."

I would soon be able to see who the riders were. They were coming into clear sight now. I bent over a baneberry bush and pretended to pick its poisonous red berries.

Good, virtuous Blackfoot girls are often out of camp, gathering berries, but they should not stand and stare at young warriors.

The rider nearest me was a short man. He rode a pinto horse. On its back I could see a blur of red, probably a red blanket. And, yes, the man's body was a thick one: could it be Dog-Leg? He had gone with Eagle-Sun. My eyes started to hurt, looking sideways like this. Who were the other two? One man was tall, like my sweetheart.

The third warrior was even farther away, on the far side of the others. I forced my eyes wider.

"It is him?" Pretty-Girl whispered behind me.

"Maybe. Stay close."

The third rider trotted forward. I drew in my breath with disappointment. He was short and thin-shouldered.

Eagle-Sun must be riding second.

The third rider wore a white man's fine long-tailed coat over his thin body. Never seen him before. I knew almost all of our people, but I did not know all the Piegan and Siksika.

Who was the second rider?

The men rode closer, down the trail that led past the river's bushy banks. I held my breath. Surely they had spotted us by now. Neither Pretty-Girl nor I dared to look. That would be too immodest.

We could listen, though. We heard the clatter of the hooves coming nearer, and then slow down. For the longest moment my heart stood still. Then the horses rode quickly on. No! I shot out a glance to see two of the horses moving on.

I heard the third. It was coming slowly, with muffled progress, through the riverside grass. I straightened up to let my face show smiling and pretended to pick berries. Where did Pretty-Girl go?

"I hope you do not mean to feed me those berries."

After more than two moons apart, these were Eagle-Sun's first words!

"What makes you think Father will give me the chance to poison you?" Something in the sound of the words tripped me. "I mean, to feed you."

We laughed at the same time. It loosened something inside me.

"We have a chaperone?" he asked.

"Pretty-Girl is picking berries, somewhere in the bushes."

"Good. I would not want you to get into trouble over this. Hear me, Sweetgrass, there is something in the wind. Dog-Leg and I brought back a Piegan warrior. He greeted us half a day's ride out of his people's big fall camp—"

"Where are the horses?" I blurted out.

"I have no horses for your father. We talked with the Piegan and rode directly back."

No horses! End of my world!

"What happened? Father will not allow us . . ."

A hard line in his face slowed me down.

"Hear me. We found this Piegan, Blood-On-Stone. He was running north, away from his people. What he told us stopped us dead." Eagle-Sun looked very worried, almost sick. "There is bad news I must tell you."

Even though Eagle-Sun was so warm and so near, I still felt somehow frightened. I looked up into his dear eyes. They did not look down into mine, so at last I had to admit that my dream was not unfolding as it should.

"Tell me, Eagle-Sun."

"I have to talk to you outside of camp this way, because of the Piegans." His voice stumbled. "When Dog-Leg and the Piegan warrior go into our camp they will ask for a council. Blood-On-Stone will tell his story, and our council will split the bands early. Tomorrow, at the latest, all the tipis will be taken down. I will not see you again till spring."

"No!" Not after all our hoping and planning and waiting.

"It is so."

We both stood silent. Wind knocked the leaves around our ankles.

"What trouble has come to the Piegans?"

"A white man's sickness has come—a stinking sickness, the one they call smallpox."

Smallpox! Here was another thing that did not seem real. Grandmother had told me how her brothers and sisters and parents and grandparents blackened with it when she was young. The disease travels on the air, just by looking. My mind slid quickly from one thing to the next.

Some of my people had gone into that Piegan camp, the All-Fierce-Wolves who went with Eagle-Sun. No.

Eagle-Sun tried to smile at me, but his dark eyes were full of sadness. I looked into them and rested my fear. What could now come to us? Our power was strong. I reached out to him.

For one shy moment we leaned close together. For the first time I touched my face to his soft buckskin shirt. It was warm and clinging. Under my cheek I could feel his heart's movement. We listened to each other's rhythms.

Eyes closed, I could not tell him from me. The blood beat through both our bodies.

The earth's strength flowed up through our feet, spread into our loins and middle hearts. We melted into one world, into everything in that precious moment. Aiii, why is our world always being hacked to pieces?

Finally Eagle-Sun stepped back. I shivered, trying to recenter myself. We must face our futures alone.

I memorized my eagle's face. Surely he had the proud daring of an eagle: strong nose, sharp eyes, sinewy hands. A ruffled eagle he was, brushing fallen leaves from his braids. He did not look at me.

Was he embarrassed by my shameful forwardness? I stood chilled by the thought. The old women would say I should not have let him touch me.

"I am sorry about the horses. . . ."

His voice was strange and wounded.

"In spring I will trade for them. I still have the trade goods. Do not worry." He bent his head so his eyes were in no danger of falling into mine. "Are you angry?"

"Would you marry an angry woman?"

"Only if she were Sweetgrass." His eyes met mine. "I was afraid you might feel I had not been a warrior and laughed in the face of death."

"You do not have to be stupid to be a true Blackfoot."

He laughed so loud his horse started, rattling the metal arrowheads in its saddle bags. We walked together, talked of little things, trying to forget the next day for a while. Eagle-Sun's horse browsed noisily on chunks of prairie grass behind us.

"Do you suppose my father might take trade goods in place of horses?"

"Maybe, but I do not think so. He does not even want to take horses yet."

"What?"

"When I sent my older brother to him, your father almost agreed I could have you. But," Eagle-Sun's eyes sparkled with teasing, "your father says you are not grown enough. . . ."

"Not grown!" I had been eligible for marriage for many wasted summers, watching my friends as they wed, one by one.

"Your father did say you were not strong enough to be a Sits-Beside-Him wife." Eagle-Sun was serious now.

Not strong enough! How could anyone . . . ? How could *my father* say that of me? I would show him.

Nightfall was near now. It was time to go home. We walked along the riverbank looking for Pretty-Girl. The sun came slanting down so golden that even the leaf mould underfoot lit into glory. Through its deadness would sprout the green shoots of springtime. In not too long. In not too long a time.

We traveled back to camp together, Pretty-Girl gratefully riding on Eagle-Sun's horse. There was nothing to say, so we spoke little. Nightfall was well over us when we reached the first tipis. And in darkness we parted.

# *10*

# THE HUNGER BEGINS

THE WIND HOWLED OUTSIDE. CURLED IN THE DEEP, dark wetness and warmth, I imagined myself like the earth, alive under the snow. Wind tore at the little sweathouse, but its round body bent too low to be lifted: I was safe from winter's blast. Outside all things were frozen stiff, but here my sore muscles were able to loosen and ache. And ache they did. I listened to their throbbing and thought: I hate you, Father.

"Not strong enough to marry, my daughter? Tell me how you would speak against that." Before he and Otter left, we had words, and each one echoed with every ache. "Let us say that a married woman prepares thirty buffalo hides in a year. Your almost-mother and you have done the ten for the tipi cover. She tells me you have both dried and scraped twenty-eight more for finishing before the spring comes. I will let you finish them, Sweetgrass. Alone.

"A Sits-Beside-Him wife has no helpers at first, you know. Without hides or meat to trade, your husband could not buy bullets, kettles, axes, good tobacco, even cloth. Maybe you would prefer to make them yourself the old way—arrowheads, buffalo-bag kettles, ground stone axes, and . . . Do you hear me, my impatient daughter? Why do you not show me how strong you are? Your almost-mother needs this help from you."

I hated my father. If I were a horse, I would bite him when he came with the saddle. How could I ever finish the hides? Only nine were done so far, and already my hands were swollen.

The gathering heat made sweat trickle down my arms and my fingers and my blisters. I poured water over the heated rocks and felt another cloud of steam burst up. It felt good. It searched out my every sore. All Blackfoots know sweatbaths give health and strength and cleanness. I wished Eagle-Sun could see me flushed rosy pink under my beautiful brown.

Everything felt better. The pain was seeping out. Oh, how I needed this. For two days the blizzard had kept us tied in our tipi. The men were not able to go out to roll themselves clean in the snow, and the women could not go out to the sweathouse. But then, this morning, the worst of the storm had passed. I said I would set up the sweat.

Winter! Every year I searched for signs it would be different. But it was always the same, always too cold. I ducked through the sweathouse opening and pulled in a handful of snow. Cold is good only against hot things. I rubbed the snow against my skin, and it melted, carrying the last terrible days off me in clear streams. My body tingled. I am strong, sang my flowing blood.

I smiled as I put on my clothes—fur underwear, fur moccasins, leggings, gown, blanket, and at last, fur mittens.

Outside, the wind had blown the clouds away, and everything shone with beauty. A hard blue sky was the earth's tipi; her snow blanket crackled with light. I could easily see the spirit of each tree and bird.

My feet moved easily across the snow. Maybe I could finish another hide today? I put my hand against the piercing shine of the river before me.

Our small river had frozen many moons ago, soon after we raised our lonely winter tipi under the dark spruce and naked poplars. Its ice was now too thick to be kicked open with a foot. For drinking water, we had to melt pails of snow. Maybe it was a good time to bring in another pailful.

The snow burned my exposed wrists as I packed it down into the deerskin bucket. There, another duty done, without anyone saying I should do it.

The men should be back by now. Father would be pleased with me for helping.

Inside, Bent-Over-Woman glanced her greetings. She all but stopped talking this last moon. The loneliness of winter always made her quiet. Grandmother, for the third winter in a row, was living with my aunt Robe-Woman's family.

The babies were no company. They slept most of the time except when Little-Brother stayed awake to listen to Mother's lessons on the correct way to speak and act. At almost two summers, he was really too young for that. Better for him to sleep as he did now, with his ruffled head on his mother's lap while she sat sewing.

I loved Little-Brother more than any of our earlier babies. Maybe he would live and grow up. Some always did.

Robe-Woman's babies often lived and grew up. My cousin Favorite-Child had several sisters and brothers. And Otter and I had lived and grown up.

Otter. Aiii. No Otter here.

No Father either. They must still be out hunting. Or had they stayed out the last two nights because they froze to death in the blizzard?

Now that was a silly wicked thought. . . .

Quickly I pulled another rolled hide from the pile still not done. Where was my rubbing-stone? Ah. I stretched the hide flat and breathed in the boiled buffalo brains used in its dressing. I worked for a while, rubbing the hide.

"Almost-Mother?"

"Yes?"

"Did Father and Otter get back from hunting?"

"Not yet."

"Maybe while I was out at the sweathouse . . . ?"

"No, they have not."

So there was no fresh meat. My stomach was grumpy. "Can I have some pemmican?"

That woke her up. "For shame! How can you ask when we have so little? You ate pemmican yesterday."

So I worked some more and held my tongue.

Finally she broke the heavy silence. "Wait until your father brings home some fresh meat—a deer, I hope. Maybe even a buffalo or an elk."

"Yes, Almost-Mother."

"My stomach is empty also. Why the elders ended our hunts so early this year I cannot understand! All men are the same. They never think of tomorrow."

Little-Brother rose up. "Please, Mother, pemmican."

Grandmother would have said yes. If the dried food was all gone, she would have gone outside and snared some small animals! I ground my rubbing-stone into the hide and pushed with the strength of both shoulders.

Maybe Father and Otter had been attacked by a grouchy bear, up before his time. Or maybe they had fallen through the ice. Such things happen.

Nonsense.

I pounded my hide again, but harder.

When Father and Otter finally rattled the tipi flap later on that night, I felt two ways—much relieved they were both alive, but oh so disappointed to see their empty game bags. They had searched and searched the woods, Father said, without seeing one creature big or small. Sifting snow covered all the tracks. So we ate a handful of pemmican without saying much, drank lots of pine needle tea, and went to sleep hungry.

As days went on, little noises started to annoy me.

For one thing, how could I work with Otter snoring? Hrrr hrrr, hrooo, hoo. I angrily ran the buffalo hide back and forth through the thong on our tipi's ridgepole. Forward and back, over and over. Would it ever soften up?

I really did not mind him snoring so much. It was just hard to work against someone else's rhythm. Why did he have to do it like that?

The baby snuffling from her cradleboard began to wear

on me too. She wanted comfort at her mother's breast, but Almost-Mother was busy arguing with Father behind me.

I ignored them. They had been fighting since Shabby-Bull woke up. Their fierce whispers flared up and down in yet another worrying rhythm, but I could not hear the words. Maybe just as well.

This hide was the fifteenth I had worked since winter began. Now it was nearly done. I pulled it out of the rubbing-thong and shook it to test its softness. It rippled in my hands like water under wind. Only sixteen more to go!

The trouble with finishing a hide is that you start thinking of food again. My stomach growled and snapped at itself. I sat down at the sudden force of the cramp. At first the work had helped me not to feel my hunger; now just thinking of another hide dizzied me.

The rubbing-thong spun around in a gray blur of motion. Here was a sign to rest for a while. What dead woman ever marries? I let myself sit quietly and dream of Eagle-Sun.

I dreamt he came walking over the snow to our tipi. On his shoulders he carried a great buck deer, its magnificent antlers dragging in the snowy ground. Eagle-Sun came to rescue us. . . . We roasted the deer over our fire. I tore juicy, savory-smelling, pink chunks of meat from the body. With my bare hands I ate it. Then the baby cried. She wanted to eat the soft pieces. I ate and ate. Almost-Mother and Father wanted to eat the soft pieces too and they fought over them. I swallowed almost a whole leg of meat while they argued. He wanted the liver, but she would not let him have it. Their voices fell, deep and menacing, then rose to shouting.

"I am going. Now!" yelled Father, his voice suddenly sharp to my ears.

That voice wasn't a dream. Father stood in the center of our tipi. He stood stiff with his arms folded very tightly, like a warrior speaking at the Sun Dance or in council. Everything else in the tipi shifted around in front of my sleepy eyes, but the upright figure was still plainly Father.

"This is our best gamble, Bent-Over-Woman," he said, his voice lower now but still harsh.

"No, my husband."

"Do what I say! Pack my extra moccasins. The river is an easy path to follow and I will not be gone long. Many animals run by the river. . . . Hear me! Do not do that."

Tears were running down Almost-Mother's face.

"If there is no game before I get to Crying-Dog's camp, then maybe Crying-Dog will give us what he can share."

"But the baby is not well!" Almost-Mother wailed as if she were already mourning for the dead.

The baby's wail was like a long, thin thorn pushed into my ear over and over again. Lucky Father, I thought. He gets to leave all this.

Almost-Mother did not give up. She loudly proclaimed that the signs were all against Shabby-Bull's effort, that there was danger everywhere. The snow is falling now, she reminded him. What if it falls thicker? There is almost no pemmican left in our bags. Bad for Shabby-Bull to go alone; bad for us to stay without him. Wolves cry lonely in the woods. What omens are there?

A warrior ought to stay with his family and see they are fed. A warrior . . .

Father moved quietly through his leave-taking ceremonies as if he did not hear Almost-Mother's pleas. Such ceremonies make good medicine, I knew. Through them, my father appealed to the spirits for our safety and his own return.

Finally he tossed a handful of dried sweetgrass upon the fire. A sudden blaze. The sweetgrass scent rose up through the flames, perfuming the winter smells of our tent. Dried sweetgrass is the fragrance of memories and power.

I squeezed my eyes shut and prayed for an escape, a tunnel through this white bleak time to the summer. Give me back my friends, a spring hill, and food enough to fill my belly. Let me be warm again. Let me smile at my beloved.

I watched the fire afterward, listened to everything, but there were no omens. Things went on as before. The wind shook the tipi walls. Our baby cried from her cradleboard.

My father walked to the opening and unfastened the flap.

"Otter?" Something quiet was said.

Otter nodded.

"Sweetgrass. Think of the hides and help your almost-mother. Do you hear me?"

"Yes, Father."

The winter swept in as Father bent through the flap. His form ghosted in the snow and he was gone. As if to answer his challenge, the wind blustered and bullied, ramming harder against the poles of our tipi. I pulled my robe tighter around my shoulders. How ever would we survive now?

I had a sudden vision.

Out in the deep darkness beyond the warm campfire, the huddled family hears a twig snap. A huge black shape rears on his hoary hind feet, stands against the purpling sky. White teeth flash. Little-Brother cries in the bear's grasp.

Hero-Woman, once called Sweetgrass, calmly packs powder into the old muzzle-loader as the others tremble behind her. She tamps the musket ball into the bottom of the gun barrel. The sheen of his fur blazing in the bloody reflection of the campfire, the bear charges. Hero-Woman dives sideways into the darkness, crouches at the same time taking careful aim.

She fires!

The bear drops Little-Brother, rears back screaming! But he lunges again, this time toward Otter and Almost-Mother. Swiftly, Hero-Woman reloads the musket and fires down the red, open, slavering throat. . . .

"We will be all right, Mother," interrupted the real-world Otter. "I will make all safe for us."

"Yes, my son. Yes, you will."

It was good that Otter had not gone away with Father. But could he really protect us against everything?

# 11

# DEATH IN THE TIPI

In the deepest part of our sleep that night, the wind died down, and the tipi's air hung still and full of change. Was that what had awakened me? I lay there uneasy. Most of the tipi was still dark, but some gray dawn light was creeping down the smokehole. It was the dangerous time.

Soft lumps poked into my back as I wiggled to get comfortable under my sleeping robes. A buzz in my head was louder than the tipi's silence. Was somebody coming?

Then the scream began. Our baby's shrill voice ripped open the dark blanket of our nighttime. Fear squeezed my chest.

What was wrong? I could hear the baby, but I couldn't see her. I shook my head and fought the webs of sleep away.

There were running footsteps and confusion and a chill of voices. Through it all the baby kept on screaming. Her voice rose and fell. I lay still and pulled my furry winter robes around me. Great shadows bent against the pale dawn light, stooping to touch the baby.

"Mother? Otter?"

They were the shadows. Good. If only I stayed still, everything would soon be all right. Mother would know how to quiet her baby. The shadows on the tipi walls bent and swayed, seemed to be untying the cradleboard cover. They freed the baby and bent to look at her.

She screamed even worse. The sound echoed sharp in my ears, like the evil voices in dreams. I sat up so I could see the baby, and see if she was really there. Maybe I was still asleep and dreaming. Little-Brother wanted to see what was happening too, and scrambled up. He toddled across the tipi, arms outstretched to Almost-Mother, who was bent over the baby with Otter. Little-Brother gripped the leather fringe of his mother's dress tight and tried to pull her back to him. They stood that way for a long time.

She did nothing. Little-Brother stood hesitating, one hand in the soft folds, until the baby wailed again, then he roared with her.

I sat straight up in my bed when Almost-Mother slapped Little-Brother. His dark hair flew outward and he fell over.

Otter picked him up under the arms and carried him back to me, saying nothing. Little-Brother stopped crying and looked at me with his mouth open. I noticed one tooth was black from eating too much honey.

"Otter?" I whispered. "What is wrong?"

"Nothing. The baby is sick."

"Sick? How is she sick?"

"She's hot. You can feel it."

My brother's eyes looked glittery to me. The rest of his face was in shadow. I knew what to do.

"You hold Little-Brother."

I slid on my fur-lined moccasins and went outside to get some snow for making water. Our babies were often ill. We washed them with warm water and made them medicine teas. Often the medicine helped them. Sometimes it did not. Sometimes they died.

It was still cold out. The snowflakes sifted through the untouched darkness around me. Drifts of them wrapped around the bare skin of my ankles like a cold and gentle fur. The forest was quiet and so beautiful.

I did not want to leave the clean coldness. The snow melted against my skin. There was almost no wind-sting to speak of. A gray dawn haze glowed over the eastern trees. Sun was coming. Sun was riding higher each day, and summer was riding close behind. Sun and Eagle-Sun.

The tipi was silent now. Almost-Mother must have stopped the baby's crying. The new-fallen snow was as hard as dust to gather. I brushed dry handfuls slowly into my bag. This snow would be clean. I stayed away from the crusted old snow underneath. No one could tell, in this faint light, where one of us might have squatted earlier.

Inside, Almost-Mother was bending over the fire, blowing at sparks hiding in the ashes. That made me feel happier. Now we would be warm. I carefully tied the tipi flap shut against the snow.

"Almost-Mother?"

She continued to blow, her face calm and cold as mountains. I scooped snow into the kettle with my stiff fingers.

"I will use pine needles. Is that good, Almost-Mother?"

But still she did not answer. Maybe the baby was very sick, and she was worried and thinking of more powerful medicines.

Our tipi was quiet now, and there were no shadows of movement cast from the yellow light growing at the smokehole.

Maybe my brother would tell me what was wrong.

"Otter, is the little one asleep?"

"This little one is asleep," Otter said of Little-Brother snuggled in his arms. "But he is hot."

Hot?

"How is the baby?"

"The baby?"

Otter did not look well himself. Not very calm, either. He held his eyes away from me. Something really was wrong with our baby.

"What came to the baby?"

"Sweetgrass, you know the way it is with babies. Any small sickness and they just . . ."

I knew it.

"She is dead," Otter admitted.

So fast? Babies die, I knew, but never so fast. When we lost the one before Little-Brother he cried and vomited for two long days. Our baby could not be dead.

But Otter nodded. It was so.

I swallowed against the dry hardness in my throat. The baby's medicine tea was still an unmelted lump of snow in the kettle. She had not even lived to see her first springtime.

· 121 ·

And now Otter said our Little-Brother was hot, too. What had come upon us?

A smell of decay, like the sweetness of too many meadow roses, wound around the familiar odors of our life. That also had come quickly. Someone must do something about the baby's body and soon. But who?

Almost-Mother still sat there beside our fire, her hands unmoving. She just sat, without cooking or counting or sewing. She did not cry for our baby, either.

She had cried for many babies, as is the way for a Blackfoot woman, but she did not cry for this one. What was different about this death? I went to her and put my hand on her thin shoulder. She shrugged it off and refused to look me in the face. To stare silent at the fire was far stranger than any mourning. If she would only cry . . .

Dawn light crept slowly down to reveal food bags, robes, a water-filled kettle, but it did not touch the dead baby where it lay. In the darkness under the slope of our tipi I could see the edge of the baby's cradleboard. There was a dark shapeless thing beside it. I took a step forward.

The death smell flowed out—strong, and sweetly horrible, like a rotting animal under a summer rosebush. Maybe it would be better if I did not look? But how was I to know?

There were many birch bark cases to feel my way between—bags of clothing, dried food, mysterious ceremonial things of power. I approached carefully, hugging my breath to myself.

Where was she? There, lying beside her cradleboard,

there she was. Of all the darkest gray things under the gray light of the farthest tipi edge, she was the only thing that was black.

She was truly black. And she was not smoothly shaped anymore either. Her tiny tummy was swollen already, puffed out like that of a corpse of many days. She looked ready to pop. Soon her shape would not be human at all.

I knew what had come amongst us, then. Only one sickness killed so fast and turned its victims to foul black dung. Smallpox. The white man's smallpox had stolen into our camp and was now bent, counting coup, over our little baby.

I stumbled out and vomited into the snow.

Next morning I awoke to Little-Brother's voice and the smell of death.

"Water, sister. Water," he pleaded, his fingers twisting the furry curls of my sleeping-robe. His fat baby face swam before me.

"Mother will get you water, Little-Brother. Go away." I let my eyes close tight again, but he kept tugging at my robe. Tiny arrows of cold shot down into me with each tug. That woke me up enough to see his face.

Tears ran down his reddened cheeks. I brushed them off with my fingers and felt why he was crying. Fever was burning inside Little-Brother, yes, and pushing out in pimply spots on his skin. These were signs of smallpox— just as Grandmother's stories had said. Why had the spirits sent this evil thing to us?

"Maybe Mother will give you a drink." It was not much to ask. Little-Brother was not quite weaned. "She does not even have to leave her warm bed." I needed a moment to wake up before going into the bitter world.

"Mother's sitting by the fire. She does not see me at all."

Aiii. Still sitting by the fire. "What about Otter, then?"

He shook his head, and another tear blotch fell from his rounded chin. "Otter's hot."

"No! Not Otter?" I sat up right away.

"Yes, and he needs water, too. He says it hurts him all over to move. Please, Sweetgrass!"

I fetched the boys some water, promised them good medicine for their fevers, and tried to stir Almost-Mother. She just sat by that dead fire and stared at it. I touched her and tugged at her and, even though it was very disrespectful, shook her a little. But she only sat with her mouth queerly puckered up, not telling me what to do.

So I did each thing as I saw it. I put Little-Brother back under his blankets, added some pemmican to the melted snow in the kettle, found a dry stick the right length for our fire, and on and on until all the tipi work was done. Still Almost-Mother would not look at me. This was awful.

"Maybe you had better take that dead baby away," Otter suggested.

How sickening, but he was right. There was no one else but me to do it, and it had to be done. The dead should not be so close to the living. I would not leave that omen of decay near Otter and Little-Brother. They were stronger; they would live.

· 124 ·

I would fight for them! Where were the blankets? A robe or a blanket is always used for corpse wrapping. I chose an old gray one and folded it lengthways and widthways, laying it down beside the body. But it had swollen now to more than the size of Little-Brother. This would not do. I hesitated, then unfolded the blanket once so it was just doubled.

"Otter, do you know how Grandmother would tell me to wrap her?"

But my brother sat hunched over, guarding his sore head with his arms. I knew he was awake. He turned his face to glare at me and that was all. Almost-Mother continued to stare at the fire.

So I pulled the baby over onto the blanket myself. Not wanting to touch her softened flesh, I tugged at the buffalo robe she had been lain on. The tail of the blanket folded down to her neck where the bottom of the blanket folded up to meet it. The sides folded over her middle and tucked into the other pieces. According to custom, I ought to have sewn them all together, but surely an unsewn blanket was good enough.

Quickly I lifted the soft gray bundle and stepped backward with it through the loosened tipi flap. Aiii, the wind blew sharp outside, but my sick lungs welcomed the clean air. Then I had another thought.

Properly we ought to move the tipi away from this death place into cleaner air. But how could I do it alone? And even if I rounded up the packhorses, took poles and hides down and moved a day's journey, how could I bring Otter and Almost-Mother to the new campsite?

I just was not able. Maybe the baby's evil spirit would

come and hurt us. All I could do was find a far tree-grave for the body.

Around our campsite grew a tall set of poplars, but they were too near. Another stand, mostly poplars and spruce, grew across the river from us, maybe two rifle shots down. They would have to do.

At the farthest end of those trees, I tied her into the branches of a white birch tree. She was so small there was no need for a death platform. I simply laid her across a pair of forked branches. The naked poplars made whipping sounds with their tops swinging in the wind. It was a lonely place, good to leave her there alone.

"Do not haunt me, little sister," I whispered before I hurried away.

The last time the smallpox came, Grandmother said, many people left their dying families and ran away. I wanted to stay here in the forest, where everything smelled clean and good, and each white branch surged with cold power. The death of the baby had fouled our tipi air.

But Grandmother said those who left died too. I thought about that as I made my way slowly back to camp. Although it was longer, walking along the river was easier going than over in the deep hard snow of the trees.

I reached a clump of pussywillow bushes growing by the river. They smelled so green, I could not help stopping. Their buds were already beginning to fill with fuzzy rabbit tail promises of spring. I poked the top of one bud to reveal its inner fur. It reminded me of Pretty-Girl's rounded belly.

I wondered where she was camping, if she was happy. Maybe springtime would let her blossom, give her some small cheer in being a mother. Springtime would also make me free—in not-too-long.

I remembered how once, when we were little, Pretty-Girl picked early spring pussywillows with me. It had been a good, warm winter, with much game. Families and even small bands were camping close together. I remembered how Pretty-Girl had frostbitten the smallest finger on her left hand and how cold it felt between my hands as we tried to warm it. We must have dropped our mittens in the snow. I remembered three of them lying on the ground, half curled, like three dead squirrels from a winter trapline. Almost-Mother scolded me later because the mittens were so wet.

Usually it had been Almost-Mother and I who had gathered the pussywillow buds in spring. She would boil them up to make a red dye. Little Otter would waste his pussywillow buds throwing them at me, and I would chase him through the bushes, both of us yelling. Then Almost-Mother would scold us.

The buds were useless to me now. The willow's bark was what we needed. As I broke off the small twigs and stripped off their buds, my thoughts returned to the ghost I had been avoiding. Had the evil that followed us here found Pretty-Girl's camp also? And Eagle-Sun's?

How does smallpox travel?

The old people say it comes with the white man's trade goods. A traveler from a southern tribe once said it was brought to his land first by white trappers, then by white missionaries. That Piegan said the smallpox had

· 127 ·

come from the far south, up the Missouri River on the American steamboat to our neighboring tribe, the Assiniboin. And then somehow it made its way to us. Maybe its evil spirit rode on the southeast wind, touched the Piegans and then touched us. Maybe it came with Blood-On-Stone, who brought us the bad news from the Piegans. Maybe it hid in our Hudson's Bay blankets. Assiniboin and Blood had traded together at the fort there.

Some even say smallpox snares you when you look at a blackened corpse. I shivered.

Who knows how evil spirits travel? Not even our wisest, oldest ones could say.

I broke from my thoughts when dull, puffed snow-clouds began to move down the mountainside. Gripping the pale green willow twigs, I turned again homeward.

The path was long and my eyes started to freeze as the cold wind swept down. The world seemed to get narrower. I walked stiff-legged across the ice to keep from falling.

Closer to camp, I scrambled up the stream's sharp banks, taking care not to drop the willow. Cold makes you clumsy. I reached shelter just as the clouds arrived with snow.

I unfastened our tipi flap with trembling fingers and swung into the warmth. It was still a stinking warmth, though.

"See what I have? Willow twig medicine to cool you off."

Almost-Mother looked at me but held on to her silence. She lay upright against a woven backrest. This would have been a good sign except that her fiery cheeks and bright eyes showed she was not restful. What if Father were dying somewhere out in the snow? Was I the last healthy person? How long would the smallpox wait to take me?

Perhaps our ghosts would drift together through the shadow land of the Sand Hills. Perhaps, but not yet. Not if I could slow it. Not ever, if I could stop it.

"Who wants willow for tea?"

Otter smiled at me, or tried to smile. He looked like a bad-dream monster. Some of the pink spots on his face had swollen to yellow pus-filled blisters, and his skin had turned reddy-brown with fever. But he smiled at me.

"Willow tea would be good, sister," he whispered. "The water should be hot enough to make it. Mother has been keeping wood on the fire."

"Good. Are you stronger?"

"I hurt so much I want to die," said Otter. "Little-Brother is very sick. Do you see him over there?"

Little-Brother was curled up on my bed, vomiting on my sleeping-robes. I ran around the fire and across the tipi to him. "Little-Brother! Stop," I yelled and almost hit him.

But the light fell across his face, and I saw strange things. In the few hours I had been away, Little-Brother's blisters had broken. They ran blood. His cheeks and his forehead were now one bloody scab.

Oh, poor baby. I had almost hit him.

I could ease his hotness, his headache, his body pains with willow tea, but nothing of mine could cure the smallpox. But I put the kettle on the fire all the same. And I prayed to the spirits. I prayed to Sun. Here are my fingers, here is my hand if you will only cure my youngest brother. Please do not let the dead baby's shadow find him. Take this sickness from his body, give me help!

Nobody—not Father, not Grandmother, nor the cruelest part of myself—would be able to say, if I lived and he died, that there was anything more I should have done for him!

But as I brewed the tea, I cried. All I wanted to do was leave all these sick people, go out on the clean snow and vomit them all away.

The willow twigs made a strong medicine. Everyone drank it. Then I heated rocks for the sweathouse and dragged Otter and Little-Brother out there. Steam is one of our long-time medicines. Many sicknesses sweat out of people—maybe smallpox too?

I boiled scraps of pemmican, roots and sour dried buffalo berries to make a soup. Soup is gentle in an empty belly. But for Little-Brother it was not gentle enough. Over and over his body rejected my offerings.

I tried again.

For several days in the early mornings, I stripped the poplars of their inner bark as high as I could reach. Otter had started to worry about his horses. So I fed his favorite horses, and Father's too. They were hobbled out in the back meadow. It meant several trips each day, my arms heaped with bark, but it was good to get out.

Otter's gray stallion always whinnied when he heard me coming. The snow was too deep for the horses this winter. They could not paw through it for grass, and they were starving. If our horses died, we would be almost *kimataps*. But maybe we would all die too, so it really did not matter.

The willow tea helped some, but not enough. It did not have enough power. Otter's blisters began to dry into scabs, and Almost-Mother's skin turned purplish as well. They drank tea and more tea, all the while slipping closer and closer to death. I did not want to, but there was only one thing left to do.

I took the dried calamus roots from my father's holy medicine bundle and began to peel them. Otter probably would have stopped me doing that, had he not been blind with fever. Never mind what my father might say later. I prepared my mind to use any of his other holy things too, if they held more power in them.

I raised each head in turn—my mother's, my brother's, the baby's small one—and poured calamus tea down each throat. A dangerous thing to do. If it goes down the wrong way, you can kill the person. But what else could I do? They all were dying. They all would have died for sure without it.

Almost-Mother and Otter looked a bit better after the medicine, but Little-Brother seemed to burn away under my eyes. Some of his scabs became stinking ulcers. Pus gathered in their edges. I washed them and washed them but the ulcers kept spreading anyway. He could keep nothing down, not even the most powerful medicines. The covers of my bed became slimy with vomit so I threw them out. I gave him some of the new robes I had been making for Father.

Summer and the Sun Dance seemed dreams of long ago. I kept looking for signs and I prayed for my father to come, but Little-Brother kept vomiting, and I had to sacrifice my last robes to his battle.

I was losing our last baby. Fear found nothing left in me to burn. I fought coldly without hope. Fighting had become my habit.

Then, sixteen days after Father left and fourteen days after the death of our girlchild, when the sun was a finger's width from its highest point in the hard blue sky, Little-Brother died as well.

And at the sun's height the next day my brother Otter raised himself from his sickbed.

At first I did not hear his words, nor did I want to. I was sitting slouched by the fire, gazing into it. It was a very fierce fire—orange, red, and deep. But he called me again and again.

"Sweetgrass? My belly hurts. Can you, can you bring me some food to eat?"

# 12

# THE RIVER DEMON

THERE WAS NO FOOD FOR OTTER AND THERE WAS NO-body to get any except me. All I wanted to do was sit and go into a fire trance like Almost-Mother had done. Our babies were dead. But if I surrendered to my lazy desire, we all would die of hunger. People coming out of sickness especially need food.

"I will find something, Otter. Everything will be all right."

Father had taken the only working rifle, leaving an old musket. No one had fired it for years. It was a flintlock like our rifle, but it used a much larger and wilder bullet. A man of my tribe once killed his close friend with a gun like that, aiming at a buffalo only a spear's length away. I saw it.

A bow and some arrows would be better, if I knew how to handle them. But then I did not know how to creep inside arrow range of an animal, either. The two skills have to go together. Using the musket was necessary.

"What do you do to this gun so it works?" I asked Otter.

My brother watched me, his eyes sparkling against his still-pale face. "You will kill yourself. Better not to ask!" He laughed and leaned back on his sleeping couch.

I did not know whether to be angry because he was teasing me or happy because he laughed. "Just tell me where the big bullets are, Hungry-Otter."

"My sister, you can stop looking. There are none."

No big bullets?

"I melted them all down to use in that rifle Father gave me."

"Aiii, Otter! How am I to feed you?"

Almost-Mother would soon need to eat, too. She had been sleeping more quietly each day that passed.

Luckily there is always gathering—the woman's way of getting food. Somewhere out there, there must be some food for us. Though where, I did not know. I picked up Otter's Hudson's Bay blanket, my woven basket and digging stick, and left.

The sun shone down through a watery sky. The air was a bit cold, but quiet. In fact, the forest was one unearthly silence, broken only by my moccasins drumming out my stride atop an icy crust of snow. Walk carefully, I thought, or you will crash through and cut your ankles. The group of poplars sheltering our tipi probably had wild roses blooming under them last summer.

I was right! Tips of several thorny branches poked through the snow. I dug down, and here and there hid withered rose hips. Thawed, the hips would be furry seeds and mushy fruit inside a brittle and tasteless skin. This meal would scratch all the way down your throat, but was welcome, so very welcome!

I gathered twigs and new little shoots from the younger trees. Many types of these boil into good, filling teas, although they are very bitter. Last I went down to the river, carrying my digging stick.

Along the widest banks were brown spikes of bulrushes as tall as a deer. Somewhere under each one were very tasty roots. But I soon found that river mud freezes as hard as rock. My digging stick only chipped the ground until it finally splintered in two.

All I got was one pale chunk of bulrush root. It looked more like a dirty icicle, certainly not much to carry home to my family.

On my way back, I spied a large white rabbit atop a hill across the river from our camp. My mouth watered as we locked eyes. But my hunger dreams were interrupted.

I heard a spooky noise, one that was new and wrong. Someone was crying inside our tipi. A woman's voice wailed out: it was Almost-Mother, sounding exactly like a woman in deep mourning.

I ran. The basket's high edge hit against my breasts with every footfall. My worst thoughts made me prickle with sweat.

I pushed everything through the tipi flap and dragged myself after.

"Almost-Mother? What is it?" Otter seemed all right.

She had not made any sound for days. She said nothing when our baby died, and did not even blink when I told her Little-Brother was gone too.

"Sweetgrass . . . Otter . . . aiii! My life, all my children," she wailed.

"What is it, Mother?"

· 135 ·

"I have always done everything properly, your father will tell you so, and nothing, nothing has ever come back to me as I tried to make it be. Otter is dying, is he not?"

"No," I said quickly, and looked toward my almost-brother. His bright eyes met mine. He looked as worried as I felt.

"Aiii!" wailed Almost-Mother. "Is he dying, Sweet-grass?"

"Look for yourself."

"See, Mother," called Otter from his sleeping couch. "I am fine."

"Everything, everything dies," she cried, "and I am going to die and so are you both and nothing of my life has made the way of anything be anything."

I pulled her body to me so that her head rested on my left shoulder and my mouth was full of her rotten smell of pus.

She was as hot to hold as a charcoal stick burning red at the core. Her cheeks shone a deep purple-brown under her stream of tears. Her thin hands fluttered over the pus and scabs of her face, blindly, fearfully, touching.

When she started calling me Shot-With-Metal, her long-dead sister, I realized her mind was not at all right. Her fever must be mounting. Maybe it would break soon or maybe . . . I stroked her hair until she lay back down. Then I washed her gently, all over.

What a sickness. Here was my almost-mother burning up while her son in the next bed was shaking under mounds of blankets and robes. Now I know what Grandmother meant when she said with smallpox there is no sleep between ice and fire.

Was she dying? I rocked her gently and pushed away the thought. Her skin had blistered lightly, not close together, and the blisters were small. I felt strange, mothering our tiny mother. But then, was I not a full-grown woman and had she not taken care of me many times when I was sick?

"Is she all right?" asked Otter.

"Yes."

"Good." Pause. "Did you find anything for us to eat?"

The rose hips and the bulrush root made a few spoonfuls of stew. Otter ate most of it. I took some in the big carved-horn spoon Father had made and teased Almost-Mother into swallowing it. There was none left for me.

That was not important, because healthy people can live without food for many days. But I had to get food for my family—good food, enough, and soon. Otherwise only I would greet my father if . . . when he returned. I chewed the inside of my lips: the blood was comfort, and the pain sharpened my thoughts.

I needed wire. Father had traded for some this summer. What was left? I searched through his bags and found a piece as long as my arm. Not enough, but it must do.

Outside, the wind blew softly. If it were a little warmer, the rabbits would wake and run. I slid my fingers down the chilly length of wire and began looking for a rabbit path. On top of the frozen stream were scattered little round scats, and some small trees nearby were nipped at a sharp-pointed angle. Ah, that soft groove worn in the snow down in the bushes. There I would set my snare.

My hands were already whitening, but I thought only of that rabbit I had seen earlier. I tied a loop in the length of wire, then fumbled its free end around the nearest poplar sapling. Finally I arranged the loop to hover over the little trail.

This is how it works. The rabbit comes hopping along his path. He does not understand what that wire is doing and is not too worried. He hops and his head goes through the loop but his shoulders hit the wire. When he panics, the loop tightens around his furry neck, and he struggles harder and harder until it cuts off his air. The rabbit dies. Then he goes home for our stewpot.

That is a painful way to go. Sorry, rabbit, but you have to die for us to live, just as shoots and grasses earlier died for you to live. So it has always been for grasses, rabbits, and my people. In this pattern is comfort.

So I thought as I dragged my weary body home to bed.

"Sweetgrass, wake up. Sweetgrass!"

My mind surfaced lazily from its cool numb dream. Someone wanted me to do something. Again. Probably something I could not do.

"What is it?"

One day blurred into the next. The mists of morning filled our tipi. Those big begging eyes looked like Little-Brother's. It could not be. They were Otter's eyes. Otter would not beg. But I knew how hunger twists inside and drives you to things you think you would never do.

Some scabs had fallen from my brother's face last night, leaving ugly pits in the skin. Who else would be pitted the next time I saw them? Inside me a deep voice answered: the lucky ones would be pitted. The others I would never see again.

"Sweetgrass? Are you awake?"

"I am now. What do you want?"

"Do you feel Mother is going to die? Am I going to die?"

I hesitated. "No, I do not feel it."

"Are you sure?"

"Pretty well. All the signs look good."

"But Mother is still burning inside."

"True, but you have both lived many days. Grandmother said that with smallpox most of our people die right away. They die and swell up like the baby." I tried to force a laugh through my tight throat. "Do you think I would stay here if you were dying?"

Otter smiled in a way I had never seen before. The softness around his eyes had nothing to do with smallpox.

"If I live, I will give you anything you want."

"Just be my good brother Otter."

He gave me his hand and I held it between mine in my lap.

"I tried to go hunting this morning," he said after a while.

"Otter!"

"You were asleep. Why not go?" he said.

"You are still too weak."

"I almost did not get out of the tipi to relieve myself. You must have been doing some dirty nursing work these last days," he said, grinning unevenly.

I chose not to tell him about the buffalo robes. When their stink became too bad I threw the old sleeping-robes outside and rolled Otter and Almost-Mother onto ones I had been making ready for Father. So no one needed to feel any shame.

"Next hunt, Sweetgrass, every second buffalo hide is yours." He knew.

"I feel I must get well now, sister. Tomorrow I will try again to go hunting."

"Your spirit is rising, but it is still tender. Just rest."

Otter would not hear me. "I can hunt with the bow and arrow and you cannot."

"Just rest."

At long last he relaxed. Luckily he was still too weak to do more than talk.

"So you must not be sad," he continued. "I wanted you to hear me, not to worry, you know, if you . . ."

If I got the smallpox.

I patted his hand and tucked him in. Otter was right. We had better be ready for the sickness coming to me, also. But he was wrong to think he could hunt tomorrow morning, or even the following morning. He must rest for many days, and most of all, if he was to care for us as I had done, he must eat well.

As I put on my mittens and prepared to go out, I thought: Why was the pox so slow coming to me? Most of the time I never thought of getting it. Me die? I would make Otter ready for it, but never would I give in! I would find power to live. *Ahksi kiwa!* My heart sang with the warriors.

I fear nothing!

There was a ghostly world lying between our tipi and my rabbit snare. The night before, Chinook, the warm mountain wind, had melted each tree's robe of snow and then blew fast away to the south. Set free for a moment, the snow-water froze again as ice. Each tree, each twig and bud wore a shining shield that the arrows of the sun bounced off, so dazzling my eyes that there seemed to be no skeletons beneath their bright flesh. This was a spirit world—a world of clearest shadows, the shadows of light.

Ax in hand, I shuffled over the icy surface crust, feeling myself the only creature in this world. Where was the flashing silver of my snare? In the snow's light, it would be hard to see, but I knew exactly where I had placed it. Right beneath those bushes bordering the stream.

The snare was empty! My heart jerked in disbelief at the sight. I shut my eyes and wished it full with a fat, white mound of rabbit.

I had to sit down. For the first time since Father left, I felt sick, really sick. A dizziness had caught me and left me weaker than I had ever been before. I had no choice but to lie back on a shiny crest of ice and let come whatever was in store.

Overhead the sun hummed down from a pale blue sky. I lost myself in the vastness of it all. The world behind me could have vanished for all I knew.

A raven's laugh brought me back. The sun had wandered on, and a light blanket of cloud overcast the sky. It was getting colder.

I took off my mitten and felt my face for spots. There were none. One small relief.

But what could I do? I could not go back without food.

And there were those hungry horses to feed as well. Frustrated, I took up our big ax and swung hard at the last unstripped poplar on this side of the stream. I cut its bark off in rings. As I pulled the inside bark from the rings like I had so often done before, I realized how weak I was fast becoming.

I threw down what strips I had gathered and picked up our bright ax. I might not have much time, I heard myself say.

I headed toward where Otter had hobbled the mares and stallions in the woods behind our tipi, inside the little meadow.

Stumbling through the fringing trees, I seemed to be in a dream where I knew what I had to do. I had to find the horses. We were starving. Horses. Meat. In this dream, the scattered tree stumps were helping me. All the tall ones were Father and the short ones were Little-Brother. But the dark figures changed back into stumps when I looked straight at them. Visions come easy when a person is sick and hungry.

Move carefully now. I must not startle the horses. Into the bitter cold of my nose and mouth crept a faint, foul odor.

Something was wrong.

From my narrow edge of the meadow there were no standing shapes to be seen, except one gray faraway blur against the trees opposite. Maybe it was Otter's stallion. Everything wavered in front of me. Where were our other horses?

A stench rode on the wind twisting through the poplars. I had to spit a lot because it made me gag. And it got worse as I went on. In the snowy meadow, I came upon a heap of gray skin and long ragged bones, which once had been Otter's horse. A leather thong still hobbled what was left of one foreleg. Aiii, the wolves had been hungry, too. The unhobbled ones must have run off.

There was no eating here.

My family's ill luck had now fully ripened. There was nothing here for me to do.

I turned on my heel and hauled my clean ax home.

I chopped and boiled old pemmican sacks for soup while Otter rested on his elbow watching me. Almost-Mother was enjoying a much quieter sleep for the first time. She was getting better, but when she awoke she would need good food. This sack soup tasted of meat and grease, but it was pretty thin. If Otter did not like it, he kept his comments to himself.

"What are we going to do?" he asked after he had eaten his share.

"There are many more pemmican sacks."

"Not enough. Have you thought about the dogs?"

"They left long ago. And the wolves beat us to the horses."

Otter's flushed skin darkened further. We sat silent together awhile, listening to our mother moaning from time to time.

"I will check my snare tomorrow morning."

On the twenty-third morning after Father left us, Almost-Mother's blisters had hardened to scabs. I held her graying head on my lap and spooned pemmican-sack soup into her. She swallowed the watery broth greedily.

For the first time, she turned her face so that her eyes could look into mine. She smiled weakly. Her spirit flickered brighter, like coals being blown on.

Somewhere I would find food for my family.

Out I crept again under the cold dome of the world. Winter was coming back again, full force. Summer seemed only a lying dream to me. I could not shake mocking memories of food eaten for the taste of it, berries thrown on the grass in laughter. I forced my moccasined feet forward. Soon I would be too weak to move them at all. Without smallpox, I might live in this way another moon or longer, hoping for my father's return. But the others would die. Aiii, already I was so lonely.

Was Father alive? Pretty-Girl? Grandmother? Eagle-Sun? The thought of them alive somewhere was a small fire to warm my freezing spirit.

The world was black with shadow, blue-white with sky and snow today—nothing else. The light shimmered off the snow, making my eyes ache. I dragged my ax behind me. If my snare was still empty, there would at least be the untouched poplars on the far side of the stream. If horses ate the green inside bark, then so could we. I found it hard to control my trembling, which came partly from desperation, partly from weakness.

I reached the snare, and its loop was empty. Always empty. So I took it apart.

My damp, mittenless fingers froze to the wire as I unwrapped it from the small tree. By the time I had the snare unsnarled, it was covered with bits of skin and iced with blood. Dragging ax and wire, I trudged up the river.

Under my feet the ice seemed to sway, and sometimes my eyes flooded with a gray fog. I would wait until I got some strength back before I went on. To walk blind on the ice is a good way to die.

Black-Eagle did that once. It was long ago, in the year of the famine. He stepped on a rotten piece of ice, out on one of the rivers in the foothills. His wives never saw Black-Eagle again, not even to bury his body. Here in front of me thrust a big stone. The dark patch on its sunny side was just like the patch Black-Eagle stepped through.

I bent over and stared into that dark ice. It was almost clear, showing water beneath its brittle frozen layers. Something moved in the darkness. With a start, I stepped back a bit. Did the dead seek me to join them?

The movement came again, and I saw it to be a black and narrow slash of a shadow, floating under the ice. As long as my arm at least. It moved sideways again. A river demon's fish!

If I fell through the ice that fish would eat me.

I remembered a story. Sometimes fish were eaten by people. Not by the Blackfoot, but others like the Cree. Our warriors called them fish-eaters in insult.

I had not heard any stories of the Cree being wiped out by river demons.

The ice was very thin here. It felt like a sign to me, the sign I had been seeking.

An evil fish waited under the ice. I would catch him and cook him. I shook with fear and power and loathing. Now.

When I hit the ax on the ice, the demon was gone like a shot. If he wanted my spirit as much as I wanted his, he would be back.

I chipped with the blade until a bowl-shaped sheet of

ice broke out. I swung the ax high and gave the ice underneath a good blow. The metal sunk in sweetly, and the water made a sucking sound when I pulled out the ax. How good to hit something!

I chipped out a big enough hole.

What to do now? I sat on a snowdrift to rest. How do the Cree catch fish?

I shut my eyes and tried to picture, one by one, my dizzy thoughts. Could a fish be grabbed? Not likely with them being so quick and slimy.

Could a fish be shafted upon an ax blade? Maybe. But when my mind pictured it, the fish split, then sank out of sight.

Could a fish be caught like a rabbit in a wire?

I opened my eyes.

I pulled off my mittens again and forced my stiffening fingers to wrap the loose end of the snare around the ax handle. It was hard to get it tight. I cut myself a few times.

The snare must go quietly into the water. I lay down on my belly on the ice.

Down it dipped into the dark hole. Success. The whole loop went all the way under the water. I was afraid I would not have enough wire. I got my mittens back on and prepared myself for a wait.

My plan was to let the fish get his head all the way through before yanking. I had a lot of time to think about it.

I never really noticed before how noisy a quiet forest can be. There is always a bird somewhere calling out to his friends. The wind is always there, rising and falling, talking to every tree. Even the ice groaned.

The ice. At first, it was just cold. Then it hurt. It sent out fingers under my blankets, up and down my spine. I got a little worried when a wash of numbness settled in, but I did not dare move or make a sound.

Then a big pointed head glided into view right under my nose. It stopped short a hand's width from my snare. Dark, cold eyes on the sides of its head could see everywhere. I did not move a muscle.

What now?

I held my breath, and he flicked his fins again. A shivering thought: fish need not follow paths like rabbits do. This creature could swim here or there or even under, and miss my trap!

I knew I had to make my move, but nothing must frighten him. Steady now. I eased the snare over the evil head so gently that it made only an arrowhead ripple where the wire parted the water.

Then the fish shot forward!

I jerked back on the ax handle. I had him!

But how well? Jumping to my feet, I hauled up on the ax handle. The demon thrashed and thumped along on the bottom of the ice before I could get his head free. Then up!

A shower of drops rained down behind him as he landed splat on the ice. His eyes were fierce and he bared a mouthful of terrible tiny teeth. Another flip, a flop, and somehow the fish escaped the wire.

I felt my entire life fall with him in that moment.

The mottled green body arched this way and that. His tail gave the ice mighty slaps, skittering him back toward the hole.

He came to rest on the jagged edge of the icehole, his

head only smelling-distance from the open water. I jumped fast to catch him. It was life against life. I sat on top of him, holding his slippery, writhing, slimy body between my legs, and grabbed his gill.

With my other hand, I stretched for the ax, caught the wire, pulled it over. Then I cracked him smartly between the eyes. I gave him another, and another.

I dared not loosen my grip until the fish was truly dead. At last it gave its final spasm, smearing blood and slime all over me and the ice.

Underneath us the river trembled. I froze. It should be a moon or more before the ice broke. Would the river demons take me?

But the air was full of nothing, nothing but a delicious slimy smell. The ice did not crack and the river did not move anymore.

I went home in triumph.


A pemmican bag thrown into the soup cut down its fishy smell. A handful of roots rounded out the taste. Mother drank several spoonfuls that evening and smiled at me again. It was a fine thing to see.

Otter drank some too and even ate flesh from the pointed bones. He said he was going to vomit. But he did not.

I ate also and went again to the river to catch another fish for my family, the next day and the next. But I went with a buffalo robe to lie on and dried seeds as bait. And I got quite good at brewing tasty broths.

No river demon took me either.

Otter's smallpox scabs fell off day by day. Almost-

Mother's blisters dried, and her face filled out and lost its shadow of the death-sign. All because of the fish.

Then came the morning of our twenty-seventh day. While Almost-Mother and Otter were still asleep, I stretched an unfinished hide on the floor and got busy with my rubbing-stone. Now I was strong enough to work some of the unfinished hides to replace the dirty ones I had had to throw out.

A warm Chinook wind spilled down from the mountains that morning and washed across the creek to shake our home. At first I did not worry. Our tipi-pegs were driven deep into the ground. Stones and ice pinned the skirts likewise. I knew we should be safe no matter how hard the wind blew.

It hit the land so fiercely the sound was almost like a creature howling. And there were other spooky noises too—scraping, thuds, and scratchings. I knew it must be dried twigs and branches kicked up against the tipi's front.

It was almost like someone dropping his packs outside, like a shadow-man fumbling at our flap to come in. Someone like a traveler . . . or a spirit.

It could not be. But I heard the sounds happening.

I leaped up and grabbed my friend the ax. There was one last rattle and the triangular flap of our door fell open. Wind gusted around my ankles and filled the tipi. A bending head and a craggy hand reached in. My breath hid scared in my throat. Was that the top-tied hair of a Crow warrior? Or was it . . .

I must stand ready. *Ahksi kiwa!*

Legs, then shoulders, appeared through the tipi flap,

and the man straightened himself. Braids lay across his shoulders in the Blackfoot way, not in any other. The face was a face I knew beneath its scarring and death-worn look.

Shabby-Bull, alive, had come home.

Smallpox wounds were pink upon my father's skin. He stood cold-face, making no welcoming sign; his body blocked the wind and the pale dawn light. He stared at the ax in my hand, the two bundled sleepers on the floor, and at the empty place where the finished hides should be.

"Where are the others?" my father asked.

"Otter and Mother are asleep, Father, and the babies are dead." It felt strange to see him, not at all as I expected.

"The babies are dead in Crying-Dog's camp as well. And so are Crying-Dog and his three wives." Father turned and tied the door flap behind him.

I pulled the blankets from the sleeping faces so Father might see them and their healing scars. He stood before them for a moment. Then he told me it was good and I was to pull the blankets up again so no one would wake.

He turned to walk to the man's place at the back of the tipi behind the fire. That limp is bad, I thought, as he dragged his left foot across the floor cover. He stopped by the kettle. Even through the stink of unfinished hides and the smoke of the fire, I could smell the telltale odor of fish. Aiii.

My heart froze, helplessly waiting.

"Daughter, what have you done?"

"We are living, Father," I tried to explain. "Otter and

Mother and me, we are living. In Crying-Dog's camp the people are dead."

He glowered at the floor while silence roared between us. Black stubby lashes rimmed my father's dark, unblinking eyes. My mouth tasted salty with blood.

"May you not mourn for this, Sweetgrass."

I knew I would not mourn, ever. My fingernails were cutting into the palms of my hands. I made myself uncurl them.

"Father, I threw out your robes. They were dirty with smallpox."

He was staring at the floor still.

"I tried *hard* to feel which trail to follow," I added, promising myself not to cry. "Father, I am not a warrior!"

"Not a warrior," he repeated, shifting his weight heavily. "But you now are a woman."

Stunned, I looked into his eyes to confirm his words. They were old, much older than when he left, but they were shining clear and proud.

"Come, give an old man a hand to sit down."

I did as he said. His weight on my shoulder, his arm round my waist were sweet indeed.

"I brought you a present. Look outside."

I could hardly see for the tears, but there on the ground by the door lay a freshly killed white rabbit.

In the sky, the sun was climbing.

# 13

# A WOMAN

"GRAB HIM, SWEETGRASS!" MY COUSIN FAVORITE-CHILD yelled behind me, as we raced laughing across the sunny prairie. We dashed over the scattered rocks and through the tall grasses. The rabbit's white tail flicked right, then left. I could almost feel my hand touch him. His tail bobbed again as he led us across a sandy space littered with gopher holes. Tricky rabbit! A foot in one of those and I might sprain an ankle.

I ran faster anyhow, knowing my strength and skill. He must have his hole around here somewhere. So it was now or never. Yesterday, Otter had caught a rabbit running. We were going to catch a rabbit too!

The bouncing brown ball skittered down a slope and turned sharply left. I flung out my arms for balance and skidded into the turn with him. He dived—Aiii!—into a thick clump of rosebushes right in front of me!

Oof! My feet were moving so fast they shot out in front of me. Sky flew up to my face and the earth hit hard against my back! Thankfully, the rose thorns had not scratched me and no one would know what had happened. A full-grown woman must only be seen acting with dignity.

As I lay on the ground, its good heat flowed up into my body, melting out the aches. The faint, sweet smell of roses mixed with dust in my nostrils while a meadowlark nearby sang her questioning song. Up past the hill there would be bagfuls of strawberries. The prairie was thick with fat animals I could snare, should I so desire. Who would not be happy?

Favorite-Child came dancing through the grass to tease me. She shook a long, thin prickly stalk at me—a foxtail bristle, with delicately cruel arrows. She poked it in my ear.

"Stop that!" I slapped it away, without looking at her.

Favorite-Child is a louse, a flea, a spider, I thought. Oh well. From the corner of my eye I could see her standing there, admiring the shiny new metal trader's ring her husband-to-be had given her.

"Where is your rabbit?" I asked.

She didn't answer. I tilted my body to the afternoon sun. If only I could pull inside me enough sun to last all life's winters . . . For sure, I was not going to get up just because of my spoiled, childish cousin.

"Where is your rabbit?" I repeated in a louder voice.

"You lost that rabbit, Sweetgrass! He never came out of those rosebushes, so he must have a hole there." Favorite-Child twisted the stem of her foxtail around and around, and tried it as a brush against her own ear.

I just lay there watching her.

"Are you not going to come with me? Otter can see us

from the top of the hill. He will tell your almost-mother if you stay here alone."

That was not true, but I would not let on. From here, we could not see his lookout place. But I knew Otter was up there on top of the small grassy hill that rose like a crooked claw out of the flat prairie. The lookout usually had scouts on it, watching for friends and enemies alike who rode toward our campsite.

In my secret heart, I knew too that Otter was watching, as a kindness to me, for a band I expected. He had promised to stand as signal if he saw the people I wanted come riding.

Eagle-Sun had sent me word three days ago that they were coming. Eagle-Sun was alive!

And I am a woman!

"Do not expect a pretty face," the messenger had said, "but Eagle-Sun has horses."

A foxtail slapped across my nose.

"Sweetgrass!" scolded Favorite-Child. "Do not dare shut your eyes and ears to me! The sun is not so high anymore. We must hurry to the strawberry meadows," said my cousin.

"No."

"We must hurry. Anyhow," she giggled, "you cannot be very comfortable. You are lying on an anthill."

What? There was a gray mound of earth, curved where my back had lain, and from its tiny holes bubbled ants— red warrior ants. Now I felt their biting. I shook myself, swatting them vigorously as I danced around.

"You look like a dog with fleas," teased Favorite-Child, and she laughed at me.

I could not help laughing too. The ants were climbing my braids and biting my ears and nose. I sat down on a big, warm rock and began to pick them off one by one. Favorite-Child pretended to help by clawing me on the bottom of my feet.

I got up and chased her. "I just have ants. You have more lice than a dog has fleas!" I yelled. We ran, with the tall grass hitting our breasts, all the way to the base of the hill. By then any ants left had fallen and scattered.

We burst into the high grasses of the lush strawberry meadow. Bits of charcoal told how the ground had been cleared by a fire a few years previous—lightning maybe, or a careless campfire. All the prairie burns sometimes and heals before it burns again.

Now purply rose-colored fireweed grew tall here, casting feathery shadows, and life grew green again over everything. Strawberries grew so thick in that meadow that I had trouble knowing where to kneel amongst them. The fire had been good to them, left them free to seek their sun.

"Look," squealed Favorite-Child. "Your knees are covered with blood!"

It was only berry juice, but she knew that. "I am a Blood woman, see?"

In this way, we happily bent and picked and laughed together, all the while keeping an eye on Otter up the hill.

There was one thing I had to say, so I said it.

"Last year at this time I went with Pretty-Girl, gathering strawberries. We had camped by the Red Deer River badlands that spring."

My cousin's pockmarked hand touched mine.

It was hot, hard picking in that sunny meadow. We filled our berry bags though, before stopping to rest. I offered Favorite-Child my largest, reddest berry.

"You are kind to me, cousin," she said, and brushed off the dust. The berry was beautiful. Favorite-Child held it up so it shone through with sunlight. "You know, we are lucky to be alive."

I thought of Pretty-Girl and her unnamed baby. Little-Brother. She-Fought-Them-Woman, my honored grandmother. Favorite-Child's father. Her brother Dog-Leg.

And others . . . there were so many others. How could I properly mourn so many?

More than half my people were blackened and gone. In some big camps everyone had died, some of them starving to death when no men had the strength to hunt. Others died because no one had nursed them. Some had hurled themselves into icy lakes and rivers to cool their fevers. They of course perished instantly. And there were those many young warriors who, in their agony and their fear, had followed their brothers under the waters. They found death the easier trail, the one for which they had trained.

We lived!

Was the way we lived a proud or a shameful secret?

Maybe someday the river demons would come for me. Who knows, but I doubted it.

Favorite-Child was still chattering cheerfully. "But then my second oldest sister—you remember, the fat one with the scar on her neck—she was luckier and only lost her children. By the way, Sweetgrass, did you hear how many are living in the camp of, ahh . . . White-Crow?"

She grinned. What a nasty friend!

"Maybe everyone," I answered, not batting an eye. "At least everyone of whom I was told." I had listened only to news about White-Crow's youngest, Eagle-Sun.

At last the meadow light turned golden, a sure omen of evening. We helped each other lift our berry bags and headed home. The sky glowed violet blue, the grasses green as after rain, and even the farthest fringes of poplar and spruce seemed caught in the clarity of their beauty. "This is how the world feels in my most powerful dreams," I whispered to myself.

"Sweetgrass," breathed my cousin softly, "Otter is standing on top of the hill."

Casting off our bags, we fell to smoothing each other's hair. Favorite-Child pulled flowering blades of sweetgrass to tuck behind our ears for perfume, and I placed several across my crimson berries. The stems would dry for sweetness for all the winter's nights.

Strong with the dignity of a full-grown woman, I lifted my burden and went forward from the scorched land, into the years ahead.

# BIBLIOGRAPHY

Chiapetta, Jerry. *Ice Fishing*. Harrisburg, Pa.: Stackpole Books, 1975.

Chittenden, Hiram Martin. *The American Fur Trade of the Far West*. Vol. 2. Stanford: Academic Reprints, 1954.

Corbett, E. A. *Blackfoot Trails*. Toronto: Macmillan, 1934.

Costello, David F. *The Prairie World*. New York: Thomas Y. Crowell, 1969.

Dempsey, Hugh A. *A Blackfoot Winter Count*. Glenbow Occasional Paper No. 1. Calgary: Glenbow Foundation, 1965.

———. *Blackfoot Ghost Dance*. Glenbow Occasional Paper No. 3. Calgary: Glenbow Foundation, 1968.

———. *Crowfoot: Chief of the Blackfoot*. Edmonton: Hurtig, 1972.

Driver, Harold E. *Indians of North America*. Chicago and London: University of Chicago Press, 1961, 1969.

Ewers, John C. *The Blackfeet: Raiders on the Northwestern Plains*. Norman: University of Oklahoma Press, 1958.

Hungry Wolf, Adolf. *Blackfoot People*. Invermere, B.C.: Good Medicine Books, 1975.

Hungry Wolf, Beverly. *The Ways of My Grandmothers*. New York: William Morrow and Company, Inc., 1980.

Johnston, Alex. "The Old Indian's Medicine," *Saskatchewan Archaeology Newsletter* 26: 1–36, 1969.

———. "Blackfoot Indian Utilization of the Flora of the Northwestern Great Plains," *Economic Botany* 24 (3): 301–324, 1970.

Lewis, Oscar. *The Effects of White Contact Upon Blackfoot Culture: With Special Reference to the Role of the Fur Trade.* American Ethnological Society Monograph No. 6. New York: J. J. Augustin, 1942.

Lowie, Robert. *Indians of the Plains.* New York: American Museum Science Books, 1963.

Mishkin, Bernard. *Rank and Warfare Among the Plains Indians.* American Ethnological Society Monograph No. 3. Seattle World Press, 1940.

Nelson, J. G. *Man's Impact on the Western Canadian Landscape.* Toronto: McClelland and Stewart, 1976.

Point, Nicholas. *Wilderness Kingdom: Indian Life in the Rocky Mountains 1840–1847.* New York: Holt, Rinehart and Winston, 1967.

Ray, Arthur J. *Indians in the Fur Trade: Their Role as Trappers, Hunters, and Middlemen in the Lands Southwest of Hudson Bay 1660–1870.* Toronto: University of Toronto Press, 1974.

Schultz, James Willard. *Blackfeet and Buffalo.* Norman: University of Oklahoma Press, 1962.

———. *Why Gone Those Times?: Blackfoot Tales.* Norman: University of Oklahoma Press, 1974.

Swanton, John R. *The Indian Tribes of North America.* Washington: Smithsonian Institution Press, 1952.

Wissler, Clark. "The Social Life of the Blackfoot Indians." *Anthropological Papers of the American Museum of Natural History.* Vol. 7, Part 1. New York, 1911.

———. "The Sun Dance of the Blackfoot Indians." *Anthropological Papers of the American Museum of Natural History.* Vol. 16, Part 3. New York, 1921.